prai

G000111624

shiny bits in between

"One of the greatest pleasures I found in reading this book was the opportunity to be so vividly and fully present in such a compelling place. I'm fascinated by the specter of a small, laid-back, tight-knit island community."

—Jessica Wilbanks
author, *When I Spoke in Tongues*

"This novel, deeply grounded in the landscape and rhythms of its particular sandy stretch of Gulf Coast, intertwines two stories of female loss. As the mystery of the connection between these stories unspools, you will be pulled deeper in, as if by an undertow. Because in these compelling stories of loss lies the possibility of renewal, both for the characters and for ourselves."

—Kimberly Meyer
author, *The Book of Wanderings*

"With a beauty for language and a strong sense of place, Georgina Key captures Bolivar Peninsula the same way Delia Owens captures the marshes of the North Carolina coast in *Where the Crawdads Sing*. A story of awakening in luscious prose."

—Maria Merrill
author, *I'm Not That Kind of Gal*

"I thoroughly enjoyed this book and felt transported to a corner of Texas with which I was only vaguely familiar. The specificity of language and the poignancy of the story lit up the peninsula for me, and I'm sure that when I next visit Bolivar, I'll see the words coming alive again in the ocean, wildlife, and residents."

—Erin McGuff-Pennington
author, "American Quartet," *Filmelodic*

"A beautiful tempest of heartache and healing."

—Tex Thompson
author, *Children of the Drought*

"*Shiny Bits in Between* is a novel about grief and forgiveness of self and others. It is a novel about living again."

—Maurine Ogbaa
author, "Goodbye," *AGNI*

"*Shiny Bits in Between* is written so vividly, it becomes a part of who you are. It's a story of the coming together of two souls through madness, compassion, and fate. Georgina takes you to that heavy place deep in your chest where you feel longing and loss. But she gently leads you with the smell of the ocean and the breeze of Bolivar to a new place of promise and light. Pour yourself a glass of wine and settle in for a great read."

—Sandra Poole

shiny bits
in between

shiny bits
in between

georgina key

BALANCE OF SEVEN
Dallas

For information, contact:
Balance of Seven
www.balanceofseven.com
Publisher: dyfreeman@balanceofseven.com
Managing Editor: dtinker@balanceofseven.com

Cover Design by Eben Schumacher
ebenschumacherart.artstation.com

Copyediting and Formatting by D Tinker Editing
dtinker@balanceofseven.com

ISBN: 978-1-947012-02-8
Library of Congress info on file.
24 23 22 21 20   1 2 3 4 5

for nan and sheila

contents

silence

*d*orie awoke to a silence she didn't recognize. Not an absence of sound, but an absence of the life she had once lived.

Birds scratched the morning air with their chatter. A branch tapped out Morse code on the windowpane. Leaves rattled against the eaves. Tires crunched over the neighbor's gravel driveway. Staccato footsteps sounded against the sidewalk as a group of children walked to school, their shouts echoing off the concrete.

But her own house was silent.

There was a time when it had been filled with noise, when her first consciousness wasn't a feeling of loneliness and displacement. Morning noises used to greet her: alarm clocks beeping, showers streaming, breakfast dishes clattering, voices scattering, doors slamming, locks clicking, the car engine fading into the distance.

Now her life was distilled down to a chair in the front room next to the fireplace, where she escaped into pages written by strangers. And to her bed, which held the promise of dreams she sometimes forgot weren't real, even after waking.

She climbed out of bed slowly, gauging the cooperation of her body, which reminded her far too often of her advancing middle age. Standing before the bathroom sink as she brushed her teeth, she tried to ignore the stranger looking back at her from the mirror with distaste. A few strands of gray hair frizzed around a creased face and dim eyes.

After pulling on loose linen pants, an old tee shirt, and sneakers, Dorie headed downstairs. As soon as she opened the front door, hot humid air engulfed her and clung to her skin. She hated September in Texas. In Seattle, where she'd grown up, September meant autumn: bronzed leaves crowned the trees, the vapor-gray sky blurred at the edges, and when she breathed, the air opened her up.

However, she needed to move her body.

As Dorie turned onto the sidewalk, a thirty-something woman walked toward her, tanned arms and legs pumping as she chatted into a cell phone earpiece. She reminded Dorie of the demented homeless man on the street corner, talking frenetically to himself or to a figment of some invisible world. From behind Dorie, the sound of sneakers pounding the concrete in a syncopated rhythm signaled a jogger, who passed Dorie with a brisk nod.

Long gone were the days when she knew all her neighbors. Even though she took the same route every day, the constant rotation of new residents disoriented her understanding of place. Anonymity replaced chats on the street, which had often led to slow morning interludes on the front porch.

Dorie passed the house being built on the corner. The new owners had torn down the quaint 1930s bungalow that had sat on the small lot, along with all the old oak trees. Now, a soulless McMansion dwarfed the lot and the houses on either side. She didn't mind not knowing those sorts of neighbors, the ones who had no appreciation for houses that spoke of previous lives through their creaks and groans, their imperfect beauty. The noise of power saws and jackhammers assaulted her ears as she continued down the street, and she grimaced at the chaos of it all.

An empty stretch of sand suddenly entered Dorie's consciousness, making her toes twitch for the grit and crunch of sand crust in place of the unforgiving concrete she had to endure every morning. Frequent childhood trips to various beaches along the northwest coast had embedded in her a visceral connection to the sea that had stayed with her throughout her life. Dorie longed to walk among scruffy sand dunes instead of these cramped urban streets.

After she'd relocated to Houston from Seattle to marry Hugh, they'd spent numerous weekends birding on Bolivar Peninsula. It was a narrow slip of land, just separated from the eastern tip of Galveston—a skinny finger stretching to reach for its long-lost sibling. High Island, a beach built on a salt dome at the eastern end of the peninsula, was known as one of the best birding spots in the country.

They had sometimes stopped in Anahuac, but it was the more secluded spots that Hugh had preferred: Smith Point and Horseshoe Marsh, during the winter months when most people were inside by a warm fire. Blue Elbow Swamp had elaborate boardwalks that Hugh had refused to use. Instead, they had scrambled through layers of gallberry holly with their bird manual, a thermos of hot tea, and sandwiches stuffed into Dorie's bag. After Harriet was born, they had tried taking her with them, but she had been too fussy.

When she started showing signs of her illness, they had stopped altogether.

As Dorie crossed the street, the door to her white room swung open. It had been a while since she'd visited the mind space she'd created to escape from and shut out the real world. She had both needed and despised it as time passed. It enabled her to switch off her feelings, to shut down her sensory perception. The antiseptic whiteness of it, the blankness, was like Harriet's hospital room—sunlight hidden behind closed blinds and replaced by an artificial fluorescent glow.

She increased her pace, her breathing hard and fast. But the familiar streets and houses of her neighborhood were now replaced by a vivid image of her daughter being ferried away in a red wagon, waving and smiling as the surgery doors swung closed behind her. Dorie's family had flown in from Seattle and gathered in the waiting area of the hospital: Her brother playing cards with his son and laughing to suppress the darkness. Her mother and father holding hands and speaking in hushed voices. Her mother-in-law fingering her prayer beads, her lips moving silently, her eyes closed in concentration. Her father-in-law hiding behind the newspaper, his leg jiggling. Her sister-in-law handing out snacks with lingering looks of concern. And Hugh sitting next to her, his eyes locked on the surgery doors.

The operation had lasted eight hours. She had felt the distillation of those hours like her empty white room, absent of any external stimulus. The compressed silence of a library, with a barely constrained current of fear buzzing below the quiet. Except for the hands on the clock above the coffee maker, which had clicked an invocation with each passing minute. Slowly, the dread had become dark creatures that crouched around every corner, peering out of the shadows as they waited for their moment.

By the time Dorie returned to the house, she was panting heavily, her heart pounding from exertion. She struggled to unlock the front door, which always stuck, and then she almost slipped on a scattering of mail that had been pushed through the mail slot onto the floor.

Dorie sorted through the usual bills and junk mail until she felt the weight of a linen envelope. Turning it over revealed the address, which was handwritten in a pretty script she didn't recognize. She sat down at her desk in the front room and reached for the silver letter opener Hugh had given her for their tenth wedding anniversary, slicing open the envelope.

The honor of your presence is requested
at the marriage of

Sara Elizabeth Calder

to

Hugh George Edwards

Saturday, the twenty-second of October
two thousand four
at seven o'clock in the evening
The Briar Club
Houston, Texas

Dorie only realized she'd been holding her breath when she exhaled with a gasp as she crushed the invitation in her hand, its pristine script distorted by the creases. Surely he didn't expect her to attend. It was one thing to accept his marriage with a semblance of grace. But to watch them celebrate their love for each other and a future together, surrounded by mutual friends, Hugh's family, and Sara's daughter?

I won't do it!

Dorie seized the letter opener in her fist and impaled the invitation. There was a satisfying thunk as its tip gouged the wood beneath. "Bastard!"

Dorie picked up the phone and dialed.

"Beachcomber Realty. This is Sally speaking. How can I help you today?"

"I need a rental house this weekend."

Sally paused for a moment. "Mrs. Edwards? Is that you?"

"Yes—do you have anything?"

"It's good to hear from you again. Time for another visit, huh?"

Dorie nodded vaguely.

"Let's see . . ." Dorie could hear keys tapping as Sally searched the database. "It's short notice, so you may not get one of your regulars."

"As long as it has a view, it's fine," Dorie said firmly.

"Ah, here we go! I think you rented this one a few months back . . ."

Dorie's muscles loosened, and she took a deep breath, envisioning an open sky over a murky sea. She'd be by the water again very soon.

little yellow house

*d*orie reminded herself to breathe as she fought the tangle of Houston rush-hour traffic on Interstate 10; she should have known better and left earlier. Back when she taught school, she had dreaded the commute every day. But that had been before Harriet got sick, when small inconveniences like traffic were the worst of her problems.

Cars and semis sped past as she reached Baytown's refineries, which resembled a sci-fi movie set. Shiny silver towers billowed white-gray smoke, and fire-breathing beasts shot orange flames into the sky. Steel cranes reached their long, skeletal necks out over the treetops to watch the cars below.

Eventually, her grip on the steering wheel loosened as she soaked in the surrounding inlets, fields, and groves of trees hugging Lost River. Once she got on Highway 124, Dorie's chest opened up as the landscape became more rural: A squat ranch-style house with two rag-and-bone horses grazing in the front yard. Another with a rusted red tractor nestled close to the house. A faded handwritten sign on the side of the road offering fresh eggs for sale.

Soon, the two-lane highway led to a steep bridge that traversed the wetlands, where leviathan barges glided through water surrounded by tall swaying reeds, swaths of ocher, and jagged rags of green. Farther along, at the bend where High Island met the shoreline, oil rigs bobbed up and down like the vintage dipping birds she'd found so comical as a child.

Dorie finally pulled onto Highway 87, a narrow road that ran parallel to the gulf along the length of the peninsula. She glanced to her left, where the ocean opened before her, and rolled down the window, inhaling deeply. The road divided the ocean and the bay, sometimes narrowing to only a quarter mile—a sliver of land struggling not to drown beneath the unfettered sea. Rows of tiny houses on tall, spindly legs lined either side, reminiscent of adolescent girls in colorful party dresses and high heels.

When Dorie arrived at her rental, she set her overnight bag in the bedroom and took a quick look around the house. It resembled every other beach house she'd rented over the years, the beige walls and coastal-themed interior making her feel anonymous. *Well, it's not like I came here for the décor.* She immediately left the house and headed to the beach.

Her stride purposeful, she traced the lace-edged water, breathing hard and deep. Salt air cleansed her lungs and cleared her head as she watched the waves mock the sand like teasing children. A hint of colder weather to come gave her a surge of energy; winter was the best season on the coast, when tourists stayed away and she had it all to herself. She dodged dips and small pools in the sand and swerved to avoid jagged wooden poles that had once held houses aloft but were now unfamiliar obstructions emerging only when the tide was low. Past lives eroded by time and tide, wayward winds, and the willfulness of the sea.

Nestled between the dunes ahead was a *For Sale* sign,

hiding amid a tangle of tall sea oats and scrubby beach elder. Shading her eyes, Dorie squinted up at a little yellow house balanced atop eight skinny wooden poles. Its window shades were half open, and it peered back at her as if trying to recognize a vaguely familiar face. She sensed its abandonment, as though she were meeting someone she knew had been left.

Dorie continued across the damp-dark sand toward the house. A sharp cry signaled that a mother bird was close by. It was late in the season for nesting, but plovers and terns sometimes lingered through early September, the cold of winter an elusive notion along the Texas Gulf Coast.

The bird hopped frantically into sight, wings fluttering, tail feathers spread wide. Dorie was stilled by its fierce maternal instinct, undeterred by her monstrous size and stumbling gracelessness. She knew that instinct to protect one's young, the strength and will to do whatever it took to keep them safe from harm. But it was not always possible. Her own maternal instincts lay dormant and atrophied.

She clambered over ragged dunes, dodging huge anthills that trailed threads of insects like strings of red sea pearls, until she reached the house. Climbing the wooden steps lightly so as not to announce herself, Dorie counted each under her breath—". . . nine, ten, eleven . . ."—until she reached the upper deck. An astringent wind slapped her face, and she inhaled its fishy, salty scent.

She knocked on the door. When no one answered, she rubbed away a small circle of beach grime covering the window. The view was still partially obscured by a hazy layer of sea muck, but the interior resembled a ship's cabin—wood and canvas and rope.

Dorie froze as footsteps climbed the deck stairs, her mind racing to find a good excuse for looking through someone else's window. She turned reluctantly to find a tall, willowy woman on the top step, digging through her purse, presumably for the house keys. When she looked up and saw Dorie, she quickly rearranged her face into a practiced smile. Dorie's skin prickled with humiliation.

"Are you here to see the house?"

"I just . . ." Dorie scrambled for the words to explain herself.

"I'm Tammy, with Beachcomber Realty. I just stopped by to check on the place." She held out her hand, which Dorie shook awkwardly. "Why don't you come on in and take a look around?"

Tammy unlocked the front door and ushered Dorie into a small sunroom. "Welcome to After Dune Delight!"

Dorie tried not to roll her eyes at the ludicrous pun. Enveloped by warm, muggy air, she inhaled a woody lived-in smell that reminded her of the junior clubhouse where she had spent her childhood summers. She would cycle past ranch-style houses, through a 1950s rendering of the perfect neighborhood. She and her friends would spend all day there, swimming and eating ice pops that melted, leaving her hands and tongue stained orange. Dorie could almost taste her first kiss—sticky sweet.

"The owner used this as a rental for years, but when the last tenant disappeared, well . . ." Tammy's voice trailed off.

"Disappeared?"

"Left . . . unexpectedly, I mean."

Dorie sensed there was more to the story, but Tammy quickly changed the subject as she led her into the living room. Scuffed oak floors and aged pine-paneled walls mellowed the light to a golden haze.

"The house was built sometime during the sixties. Probably moved from one of the nearby rural areas—there was a lot of that in these parts."

Dorie imagined the house being raised high in the air by cranes, dangling precariously from a series of pulleys. They would have had to aim just right to balance it atop the stilts, as the house took time to settle solidly on its new foundation.

Dorie forced down a gasp as she entered the kitchen, where a massive window dominated the room, framing the expanse of sea and sky, a hoary cloth thrown over the world. Tarnished light flooded the space, creating the impression that the inside and outside worlds were colliding.

"I know. The view's spectacular, isn't it?" Tammy gestured to the metal sink and countertop that extended the length of the room. "The original owner installed this from a ship's galley. See these latches on the drawers? That's so they wouldn't fly open during storms."

Well, hopefully that particular function won't be necessary. Dorie fingered the latches—ancient locks hiding the mysteries of past lives, lives that had left their mark on this place. If she were to live here, would the house guide her journey like a ship on the water? Or would she stand purposefully at the helm and steer, determining its course?

"It does, of course, come furnished."

Tammy swept her arm out to encompass the living room as they headed toward the bedrooms. Dorie took in the wood-framed sofa threaded through the base with fishing rope and a table shaped like a ship's wheel. *Thankfully, that can be changed easily enough.*

"So, there are two decent-sized bedrooms, plenty of room for the family. How many are you?"

Dorie kept her back to Tammy. "Just me."

"Well, I'm going to let you poke around on your own for a little bit, get a feel for the place. I'll be outside when you're ready."

Dorie's initial instinct had been correct: the interior

resembled a boat, with its compact rooms and proliferation of wood and filtered sunlight.

When she joined Tammy outside on the deck, Tammy blazed her hundred-watt smile again. "So what do you think? It's priced to sell!"

Dorie looked at the house once more and then turned to the expanse of ocean before her. Perhaps it was time to press her own reset button.

Dorie sipped coffee on the deck of her weekend rental while finishing the crossword she'd started that morning. She gazed in the direction of the little yellow house by the sea. Her Houston house would surely sell easily; the market was strong right now, and the growing gentrification of her Houston Heights neighborhood meant she'd get far more than what she still owed.

She and Hugh had halved everything right down the middle when they split—a highly amicable arrangement. Hugh was always insistent on being fair and generous to a fault, a quality that Dorie had struggled with as it tended to enhance her own flaws. She had gotten the house in the divorce, and he had kept his 401(k). Still, it was a challenge to pay the bills on a freelance editor's hourly wage, especially when there were gaps between jobs.

She began scribbling in the margins of the newspaper, working some numbers. She could pay off her loan and put a large down payment on the yellow house, which they were practically giving away. Her pulse quickened, and her stomach fluttered with possibility. John would probably agree to send her jobs now and then since she worked from home most of the time anyway. Besides, Houston was only an hour and a half away from Bolivar; she could easily drive in when necessary.

A seagull landed on a wooden post next to her, its sharp yellow eye like amber glass. *What are you telling me?* she thought as she met its gaze. *Is my life of my own making, or did fate lead me here? Certainly not all the events in my life are of my choosing. If they were, Harriet would be here on this deck, watching the seagulls soar and sing.*

Although it had been four years since they'd lost her, there were still moments when it felt like only days.

"Tell me," Dorie asked the bird, "what am I to do with the remnants of my life?"

Opening its wings and calling her name, it flew toward the crashing waves made dingy by the clouds overhead: *Dorie, Dorie . . .*

voyeur

onths later, the little yellow house no longer resembled a ship's cabin. The late-winter sun filtered through the shades, veiling the room with diffused light. Now-vacant spaces had replaced the old couch, chairs, and table, which Dorie had taken to the resale shop.

Now that it was gone, she realized the furniture had belonged to this place in a way her own did not. The hefty mahogany chest filled with vintage linens her mother had given her looked cumbersome at the foot of Aunt Edna's high antique bed in the small bedroom. Books, lamps, and artwork she'd collected over the years were scattered randomly throughout the house, waiting to find their place.

The only furniture she'd kept that had come with the house was the wooden table and four chairs by the kitchen window. A shard of pale light divided the pitted wood. *They are the only things that belong here.*

She'd spent most of the day unpacking and needed a well-deserved break. Unfortunately, Rennie, the handyman she'd hired before she moved, was still doing some repairs on the exterior of the house and refreshing the yellow siding. She cringed at the off-key notes coming from the deck outside the living room window. Even with all the delays in selling her Houston house and then buying this one, Rennie still wasn't done, having made some excuse about bad weather delaying the job. Dorie had been forced to move during the holidays, and she felt a tinge of melancholy as she looked at the half-empty living room, void of any festive spirit, not even Christmas lights.

But then, she hadn't celebrated Christmas properly for years.

When Harriet was young, they had enjoyed a tradition in her old neighborhood. A Saturday in December had been designated for neighbors to stroll through the quaint streets, where houses were lit up and decorated with garlands and wreaths. A few even had carolers and small concerts on their front lawns, with offerings of hot cocoa and fresh baked cookies. She had loved the chill winter air on her skin as she pulled Harriet in her red wagon.

When Harriet was about six years old, she had started to find the tradition exhausting and would usually suffer a health setback of some sort, so they had stopped going. They spent Harriet's last Christmas mostly at the hospital. MD Anderson had been determined to bring cheer and goodwill to the pediatric ward by hanging garlands and lights and hiring a Santa to pass out gifts. But it had taken everyone's strength just to smile.

The ring of a cell phone just outside her window interrupted Dorie's memories. "Yep. Sorry, Shel, but it looks like I may be a tad later than I said. . . . Don't worry. I think I can get the car before the shop closes up."

Is he always late for everything? She went to the window and peeked through the blinds. Rennie was grimacing as he presumably got an earful from whoever he was talking to. Well deserved, she was sure.

"It won't be seven before the kids eat; I'll make sure of that myself. How about I cook? We could fry up that fish I caught the other day." He paused, his face smoothing out. "She's okay. Just a bit testy, like you sometimes." Dorie flushed and backed away from the window. "I know, I know, but the fish were calling, Shel—a temptation way stronger than a day's pay, let me tell you."

I'll bet! We'll see how much you appreciate a paycheck when I fire your ass.

Grabbing the newspaper and her full mug of tea, she struggled to open the front door with her hip, almost smacking Rennie in the face. He mumbled into his cell phone and quickly hung up.

"Dammit!" she barked as piping-hot liquid sloshed onto her hand. She pushed past Rennie and sat down at the table, hunching her shoulders as she peered at the crossword.

"You okay there?" Rennie asked.

Dorie grunted and attempted to concentrate on the crossword, tapping her teeth with the pencil as she tried to ignore Rennie, who had thankfully returned to his work. *Two down: Quick witticisms (7).* Her mind went blank; all she could think about was Rennie interfering with her solitude. If he started singing again, she'd be forced to gag him indefinitely.

It was no good; she couldn't relax with this stranger on her deck, interrupting her peace and quiet. How was she supposed to settle in and make this her home when she had to share it with him?

Dorie had unpacked most of the moving boxes, which were still strewn about the house, hollow and discarded. But she remembered seeing a few strays down in the garage, so she abandoned the crossword. She glanced at Rennie, her mouth a thin line, before clomping down the stairs.

Musty air enveloped her as she opened the heavy wooden door of the garage and peered through the dim interior. A huddle of boxes leaned against the rear wall. She tugged at one of the warped box flaps to reveal piles of paperback romance novels and mysteries. They weren't her boxes after all and must have been left by the previous tenant. After opening a few more and shuffling through old receipts and ledgers, Dorie decided that, more than likely, she'd need to toss them. Yet another annoying task she'd have to get to before finally being able to relax in her new home.

When she pulled open the top of the last box, though, she found a book with a brown leather cover mottled by sand and humidity. She picked it up. It felt swollen, as if it were filled with more words than could fit within the confines of the binding. A piece of paper slipped from between its pages: a pencil sketch of a young boy with gentle eyes and a sweet smile that made her swallow hard.

Dorie opened the book with a sense of anticipation, as if she were meeting someone she suspected may become important in some way. Written on the inside cover was *Clementine del Castillo*. Perhaps it had belonged to the previous tenant Tammy had mentioned. Dorie wondered why she hadn't taken it with her when she left. The pages were thick with ink, words and doodles crammed onto every surface so they rippled and dipped, as if the writer had painstakingly etched herself into the fabric of the paper.

She suddenly saw herself from afar, a voyeur excavating long-buried secrets. Dorie closed the book, heart thudding in reproach. Her hand hovered over the open box, the journal wanting to be dropped back into the darkness again. Instead, she pulled the book close to her chest and exited the dusky light of the garage.

When Dorie climbed the steps to her deck, she was surprised to see Rennie hard at work. She'd half expected to find him sitting with his feet propped up on the railing, taking a siesta.

"I should be able to knock out the rest of this topcoat in a day or two, and I'll be out of your hair."

Dorie stood before him, arms folded around the journal, mouth firm. *It had better not be more than two days, or else,* she promised herself, while simultaneously worrying about how she'd find someone new on such short notice.

"I'll expect to see you bright and early tomorrow morning, then." Before he could respond, she entered the house and closed the front door.

Dorie sat down on the couch and stared at the journal in her lap for a minute before opening it to an entry near the beginning.

March 11, 1998

Bolivar is a world away from the life Lou and I had before. The relative seclusion and quiet are a relief after the constant buzz of Houston. But I wonder if we thought it through enough. Rushing to move in before Lou's next rig job may not have been the best decision. We just wanted to be together as much as possible before he left. I blocked out his pending departure until the very last minute, when he left with a bag slung over his shoulder. And standing on the deck yesterday, watching him drive down the dirt track and take a right onto Highway 87, I ached for him. Today was a buried blur of sleeping too much, reading, and walking on the beach. I can't paint. I'm too preoccupied with the metallic pain of missing Lou's voice and hands.

I've learned the rhythm of his comings and goings, which mirror the ebb and flow of the tide. We write countless letters back and forth to each other so our thoughts, at least, can mingle close when our bodies can't. But then I become bored and restless and set up a new canvas and paint until I get lost in a landscape of my own imagination. Last week, when he walked through the door calling my name, I was confused, having forgotten our love for each other.

He loves to watch me paint. Starting with a blank canvas, then abstract maps of charcoal lines that grow more complex as I add light and shadow. Next come blobs of color on my palette, blended and layered onto the canvas. He says I create a life, a landscape or a person painted into reality, and he wants to know that place or that person intimately.

When I have one of my sleepless nights, my mind roaming to the dark edges, where my mother is nothing but the sharp horizontal blade of my father's suited shoulders as he stands with his back to me—I turn to Lou and stroke his face until he stirs. He mumbles and rolls toward me, burying his nose into my neck, inhaling my sleep scent. I feel guilty for waking him, making him share my darkness. He strokes my back and sings Johnny Cash into my ear, until my father recedes and is replaced by the light.

She was an artist. Dorie wondered if any of her work was still in the house somewhere.

She became aware then of Rennie's truck fading into the distance, so she poured herself a glass of wine and went to sit outside, where she could finally enjoy herself in peace. A number of oil rigs lay scattered across the horizon like a string of half-broken Christmas lights. Shame to think what potential ruin they might inflict on the coast. It was bound to happen eventually, though. Would it happen in her lifetime?

What would the landscape look like decades from now? Undoubtedly, her house and those around her would be gone, wiped out by a hurricane or simply erased by the sea as it reclaimed the land. Her mind started to wander into a dreamscape filled with blue-green water, where fish glided past, hovering over the pages she read like her cat used to, competing with the tangle of words.

A night breeze grazed her cheek, bringing with it a haunting moan that mingled with the sound of the waves below. The moon was full and low in the darkening sky when her half-closed eyes registered movement. Fluorescent-green light darted through the waves. And again, but this time, it moved across a stretch of water, a living creature with a purpose, spreading out and then merging again. The green light undulated and jumped, multiplied, skipped through the waves, and then disappeared. Dorie's skin prickled as her mind raced for an explanation: mermaids, aliens, sea spirits?

Harriet?

It had been a long time since she'd looked for signs of Harriet in everything she saw, possible threads leading to her daughter. She used to obsessively search for meaning in patterns, dates, rearranging numbers of every combination: lottery tickets, missed bus numbers, the significance of the day and time Harriet died.

The green lights in the waves flickered in time with her rapid calculations: Harriet's birth date—10/8—minus the date she died—5/6—was the hour she died (18–11=7). May 6 at 7 p.m. Perhaps she should go down there and open herself up to her. But that was crazy; of course it wasn't Harriet. Although—

As suddenly as the green lights had appeared, they disappeared again, and Dorie was wrapped in darkness. Even the moon was only a smudge behind a sheath of clouds.

She stood, chastising herself for being so foolish. *Don't let yourself go back there,* she thought as she got ready for bed. When Harriet had gotten sick, Dorie hadn't been able to sleep anymore. She had taken sleeping pills for a while, but they had stopped working. So she had decided to stop fighting it and learned to find a strange form of solace in that liminal space between dreams and reality. Where real life stopped and she hovered on the periphery of this world. Where her mind could wander without interruption, meander through her memories, and visit what might have been. Hugh had told her it was a dangerous place to live, but it suited her fine.

bolivar peninsula

*t*he full moon scorched the water where Clementine entered the sea, clusters of sargassum tangling about her legs, the hair of wayward mermaids tethering her limbs to the shifting sand. Her arms waved gently among the darting green lights that guided her as she called to the moon, a lament for her lost boy. Moving deeper into the shining water, she listened for him, following a shoal of tiny fish—a hundred drops of mercury. She read the currents that swerved and flowed, the detritus of the ocean floor revealing its secret code like braille. Leading her farther, deeper, closer to him.

phosphorescence

orie became aware of tears on her cheeks as the final remnants of sleep dissolved. Dream images slowly faded: flocks of birds keeping watch over wailing mermaids who shed glowing tears of phosphorescence that got lost in the sea. She opened her eyes to early morning light, disoriented by the still-unfamiliar surroundings. Mermaid song blended and morphed into another jaunty tune, courtesy of Rennie, outside her window.

Wanting to enjoy the cool sea air, she went out to the deck, determined to ignore Rennie and read more of Clementine's journal. She flipped through the pages, stopping when her eyes caught on the word *baby*:

September 14, 2000

I felt the baby kick for the first time today, and I waited for another, watching my belly ripple as his foot rolled beneath my skin. I'm inhabited by this tiny being, my body not my own. But I give all of myself to him. Before Finn emerges into this world Lou and I have made, it will be me who nourishes him and me whose heart beats in time with his. Soon, he will move into the light, into this place where wave song will be his lullaby and the salty ocean his baptism.

She had a child. Perhaps the boy in the sketch. Dorie flipped through the pages closer to the middle of the journal, searching for another reference to Clementine's child.

May 15, 2004

Curtis caught a shark this morning, and Finn was mesmerized. He asked why it wasn't moving, decided the bucket was too small, that it wanted to return to the ocean. I watched its gills heaving, its eyes cloud over. A thread of red trailed its feeble attempts to escape, tethering it to its fate. Finn finally walked away, head down, searching the sand for triangular shards of black, as Curtis had taught him. Whenever he finds a shark tooth, he puts it under his pillow so the tooth fairy can reunite it with the ghost shark, which will make it "oh, so happy." He so wants everyone to be happy.

I fail him. Sometimes he sees me cry, and I hate myself.

Finn. And she had mentioned Curtis, her neighbor. Dorie had met him during her many visits to the area over the years. She'd have to ask him if he knew what had happened to Clementine.

"Today's another beauty," said Rennie, sitting back on his haunches and picking up the mug that sat next to his thermos.

Dorie kept her eyes fixed on the journal. How had Clementine failed her son? Perhaps everyone thought they had failed as parents. Dorie knew she did. When Harriet was sick, she had felt impotent. The only way she could begin to cope during that time was to fool herself into thinking she had some control over Harriet's illness. She had thought that if she kept on top of the doctors to make sure they were doing everything possible, paid the hospital bills, called the insurance company over and over, researched alternative treatments when the standard ones weren't working, made sure Harriet had her chemo even when she begged Dorie to stop it—then they could beat the cancer through sheer will. She had thought she was being strong for her daughter, but mostly she had been avoiding the truth that they might actually lose her. So she had forgotten to just be with her, to make sure Harriet saw how much she cherished every last moment.

Rennie continued his attempts at conversation, undeterred by Dorie's dismissals. "Hey, did you catch the light show last night?"

Dorie started. *So I didn't imagine or dream it.* She turned to look at him. "What was that?"

"Bioluminescent plankton. Pretty cool, right?"

"Plankton? But it looked so . . . magical . . ." Her voice was that of a child discovering Santa wasn't real.

"Well, sure. Remember when you were a kid chasing fireflies? I'd spend hours with my friends collecting jarfuls of them. Kept them in my room so it lit up like Christmas in July."

"I used to convince myself they were fairies." Dorie remembered the shoebox house she'd once made for them, painted green with cotton-spool tables and thimble chairs, decorated with the tiniest flowers she could find. It wasn't until Rennie responded that she realized she'd spoken aloud.

"Exactly. Magical."

"Yes, but they weren't fairies, were they? And I'm guessing you ended up with jars full of dead bugs."

Dorie turned back to the journal in an attempt to avoid further conversation. Rennie put down his mug and reached for the paintbrush. Glancing out the corner of her eye, she watched him dip it into the tub and apply bright-white paint to the window trim. It contrasted pleasantly with the fresh yellow paint on the exterior walls, and a ripple of satisfaction lightened her dark mood slightly.

He painted with meticulous care, as though stroking a sickly dog back to health. She wondered how old he was. His face was lined, his hair slightly graying but still thick. He was tall and lean and held his body with such ease that Dorie longed to assume his shape for a little while, just to see how it fit—limbs loose, muscles strong, a body capable of living life easily. They remained quietly for a bit, until the sea breeze nudged her and the waves beckoned.

As she made her way down the stairs, she caught sight of what looked like a cat darting out from the outdoor shower enclosure. It stopped and eyed her for a moment, as if deciding whether Dorie was worth befriending.

"Don't you go getting any ideas," Dorie said out loud. The cat moved hesitantly toward her and began to rub against her leg. "Oh, no, you don't. I'm not falling for that trick. Shoo!"

She waved it away with her hand and headed across the dunes to the beach, anticipating the cool chill of water on her feet. The cat scampered into the tall grass, probably in search of crickets or mice.

As Dorie drew closer to the shoreline, she saw an image drawn in the sand: a yin-yang symbol. She wondered who had drawn it and why. She'd become fascinated by the ancient Chinese philosophy of dualism while teaching her writing students about it one year. The idea of two separate but complimentary forces that must balance one another to achieve harmony was something she strove, and usually failed, to achieve. She thought of her white room and of the darkness of night that had become a solace of sorts. Her acquiescence to the nocturnal meanderings she'd adopted to cope with her chronic insomnia allowed her mind to wander. She often entered another state of consciousness, though not always one she wanted to inhabit. Light and dark, a necessary balance, a necessary escape.

After her walk, Dorie passed by the garage, and it occurred to her that perhaps there might be more of Clementine's journals in there. As she dug through boxes filled with layers of paper, her pulse quickened when she found a number of letters addressed to Clementine, most of which were still sealed. On many, the return address in the top-left corner read *Texas State Penitentiary at Huntsville, c/o Lou Walker.*

Dorie tipped the entire contents of the box onto the garage floor, searching for clues to this woman who had once lived in her house. Her eyes sifted rapidly through bills and paperbacks until they landed on more envelopes, which she pulled out and stacked in a separate pile. She picked up one that was torn open and slipped the letter out, slowly deciphering the hieroglyphic scrawl.

August 21, 2001

Clem,

I've been calling you for weeks! Where are you? Why aren't you picking up? I got done with a rig job a few days ago and wanted to see you. I'm getting really worried. What's going on? I know things haven't been good with us for a while, but I don't want to lose you. I'll make it up to you. And to Finn. Give him a kiss for me, and know I'll be home soon and that I think about you both every day.

Lou

Dorie held the page up to her nose and inhaled, wanting to know something of the person who had written it. She smelled mildew and the faint remnants of stale cigarette smoke. She threw armfuls of the discarded pile back into the box and collected the bundle of letters in her hand, hurrying back upstairs.

beauchamp ranch,
bolivar peninsula

*C*lementine crept silently into her room at the ranch, not wanting to awaken Agnes and Earle, to see their faces furrow and sag with her despair. She removed her sodden clothes and lay rigid on the bed, the worn springs mimicking the groan of her bones. Finn's shell still hung around her neck, the tiny barnacles that sprinkled its surface scraping her skin. She dipped her forefinger into the crevice that led to the dark curl of ivory and imagined an empty chamber now inhabited only by ghosts.

Where did the waves carry this treasure? Did the once-living creature that inhabited it tread the ocean floor, its imprint lost in the murky depths, where no one would ever find it? Did a deep-water current toss it up so it was caught in the rush, carousing with silver fish and tentacled beasts who swept it closer to the surface so he could find it for me?

The green lights she'd followed in the waves that night had taunted and flickered, led her astray. But he had stayed silent. She'd heard his cries once in the moon-scorched water. After she'd sprinkled his ashes there. But no more.

I must go to where I first lost him. That is where he'll be, waiting for me, wondering where I am.

It was time to leave this place of too-soft whispers and eyes that watched her breathe. Eyes that watched her sleep, the first sight she saw upon waking. Agnes and Earle could not bring back the light.

Only I can do that.

coconuts

Now that Rennie had finally finished the job and Dorie had the house to herself for a few days, she realized she needed to be among living, breathing people, rather than just reading about them on a page.

Walking into Coconuts was like taking a step back in time. The anachronistic odor of cigarette smoke fugged the air, mixing with old wood and fried food. Her urge to mingle wavered a little, though, as she sat at the only free table. It was near the bar, where men in mechanic hats and oil-stained overalls stared mutely at a baseball game playing on the TV.

"I'm Shelley, and I'll be serving you today." The waitress was a too-skinny brunette wearing a tousled ponytail and cowboy boots to offset her standard uniform. She seemed a bit worn out but was doing her best to be cheerful as she handed Dorie a menu. "Can I start you off with a drink? A beer? Our margaritas are real good."

"No, just an iced tea, thanks."

"Sure thing. Take a look over the menu, and I'll be right back."

Country music played in the background, and a couple at the next table started singing along. Shelley looked over at them as she headed to the bar, her brow wrinkling.

A woman with very long blonde hair motioned the waitress over to the bar. They spoke in hushed voices, occasionally glancing back at the singing couple, whose voices were growing louder as the chorus kicked in. Dorie decided that staying for lunch wasn't worth having to listen to the tipsy songbirds while trying not to breathe in cigarette smoke. She'd get her order to go.

Her attention was suddenly diverted as a familiar voice sounded from the entrance.

"Don't start acting all crazy on me. Your mom'll kick my ass if you start running around in here!" Rennie, carrying a large cooler, followed two rambunctious boys into the restaurant. He headed over to the bar and dumped the ice chest on the counter, calling out to the waitress. "For you my dear: this morning's catch and dinner for a week or so."

Shelley's face brightened. "Why, thank you!" Then she frowned as the boys began heading for the kitchen. "You boys stop right there; kitchen's off limits!" She motioned to Rennie, who handed the boys some crayons and kids' menus and sat them both on stools at the bar. "Where's Izzie?"

Rennie shrugged. "Wasn't there when I picked them up."

Shelley's face hardened. "I'll kill that girl, I swear."

Rennie leaned over to the blonde and gave her a warm hug. "Howdy, Lynn. Good to see you! Hey, Shel, want to share?" Rennie winked as he started to open the cooler.

Lynn laughed. "Oh, that's okay. Ken went out this morning with Pete, so our fridge will be good and full. But thank you anyway." She linked her arm through Rennie's, silver-and-turquoise rings flashing on almost every finger. They continued chatting as Dorie tried to concentrate on the menu so she could order.

"You decided?" Shelley asked, smiling down at her.

"I'll get the crab cakes to go."

"All righty," Shelley said.

That's when Rennie noticed Dorie and strode over.

"Good to see you out and about." He stood before Dorie with a wide grin on his face, his hands in his jean pockets as he rocked back and forth. She smiled back awkwardly.

"So who's this?" Shelley asked.

"Oh, sorry—my manners. This is Dorie; she just moved here. I finished painting her house last week. Dorie, meet Shelley."

Shelley rolled her eyes. "Oh, you had to put up with my brother for far too long, I hear."

"Yes, well, it's done now, so . . ." Dorie faltered, thrown by the unexpected discovery that they weren't married, as she'd assumed.

Rennie was still smiling. "I apologize, but you're going to have to get used to beach time. Things move slower in these parts, for sure." Even his voice moved slower than most. It seemed to force her to breathe more deeply.

"I'm afraid fishing trumps most things in Rennie's life these days." Shelley put her arm around him affectionately and smiled, patting his shoulder. "Except us, of course."

"Hi, there. I'm Lynn!" The blonde joined them and held out her hand.

Dorie took it reluctantly. "Dorie." All three of them stared down at her, and she suddenly felt like a specimen on an examination table.

"Lynn owns the lighthouse here on the peninsula," Rennie said.

Dorie had admired the tower since she first spied it from the ferry years ago. Most tourists rode the ferry from Galveston to Bolivar and didn't even bother getting off the boat before backtracking to Galveston again. In fact, many weren't aware there was a community worth exploring on the other side.

Lynn gathered her hair into a messy topknot. "So, you're new here? Well, it sure is nice to meet you. Any friend of Rennie's is a friend of mine. We need to show you around, introduce you to some neighbors. Isn't that right, y'all?" She beamed at the other two.

Dorie tried to smile. The couple at the next table had stopped singing, but the man was standing up on unsteady feet. He attempted to drag his lunch date from her seat. "C'mon and dance with me, baby. You know it's my favorite. You gotta dance with me. I'll hold you close, real close." His molasses voice was slurred and thick. He was so skinny and tan, he resembled a mesquite tree, stark and twisted in the parched Texas panhandle.

Rennie moved over to the man. "Come on now, Walt. Take it easy. I don't think Lisa feels much like dancing right now." He kept his voice low and touched Walt firmly on the shoulder.

"Sure she does—don't you, Lis." He continued trying to pull her up from her seat, where she was starting to look uncomfortable.

Rennie took out his wallet. "Hey, lunch is on me. Why don't you guys take the party back to the house."

Pausing for a second, Walt looked bleary-eyed at Rennie and then slapped him on the back. "Thanks, buddy. I owe ya!" Then he made his way toward the exit. "Yep, time for us to get outta here. Let's go, Lis; I'm gonna show you some moves when we get home. You better believe it!"

Lisa got up and gave Shelley a look as if to say, *Don't worry, I can handle this,* and Shelley nodded in recognition. After they'd walked out, it occurred to Dorie that neither of them should be driving. But it seemed the rules were different here—or else everyone just ignored them.

Shelley's boys ran over, giggling. "He was funny!"

Shelley shook her head. "Rennie, can you take Johnny and Chase home please? And I'd really appreciate it if you could try to get hold of Iz."

"Sure thing. I'll see you later, Dorie. Let's go!" Rennie rounded up the two boys, pretending to be a shark as he chased them toward the door, humming an ominous tune. Once he'd caught them, he wrapped them both in his arms, pausing and speaking quietly in their ears to calm them.

Lynn was leaning toward Dorie with a pen and paper in hand. "It was great to meet you. Why don't you give me your number, and we'll plan something." Dorie wrote down her number using her messiest writing so Lynn would maybe misread a digit. Dorie wasn't sure she could handle someone who smiled way too much for her own good. Taking the paper from her, Lynn said she'd be in touch and walked back to the bar, where Shelley was ringing up Dorie's order.

Dorie put a twenty-dollar bill on the table and took the to-go bag from Shelley as she approached. "Keep the change," she said in a voice that she hoped sounded friendly and relaxed and tried not to walk away too quickly.

When Dorie arrived home, she was greeted at the bottom of her steps by the stray cat, who meowed at her pitifully. She opened her to-go bag, broke a small piece off one of the crab cakes, and held it out. The cat devoured its feast and meowed for more, nudging her hand. Dorie stroked its fur, which was

35

riddled with fleas, its spine hard ridges beneath her fingers. She took out the rest of the crab cake and put it on the ground.

"It's good, huh?"

She marveled at how the cat purred and ate simultaneously. *It's very friendly for a stray,* she thought, watching it eat. Dorie thought of the waitress, Shelley. She and Rennie did resemble each other, both lean and slightly crumpled, but in a good way. As though they were comfortable in their own skin and didn't fuss too much over every detail of their appearance, much like the scruffy tabby before her. She'd always been a bit suspicious of people who were too well put together, too perfect, as if they were trying too hard.

The rest of the day was spent organizing books on the bookcases, relishing the peace and quiet. When she and Hugh had first moved in together, their library had been almost unmanageable and had included several duplicate copies of their favorite books. She found great pleasure in reaching for a book splayed open on the bedside table each night, marking her progress through the vicarious life she led through its pages. She loved the heft and the leathery softness of a page turned by countless fingers.

Dorie picked up a tattered copy of *The Lion, the Witch, and the Wardrobe* from the top of one pile of books. It opened easily to the passage where the young heroine first entered the wardrobe that led to a magical land—Harriet's favorite part. After reading it for the first time, she had checked every wardrobe she encountered.

"You never know," she'd say, her tone becoming more humorous as she got older, her huge round eyes betraying her naive hope for another chance at life. Harriet had dreamed of that magical place where she could live an entire lifetime before returning to this one. She'd known by then that this life was not the version she would have chosen.

Dorie hugged the book close, feeling her daughter in its pages.

The peace and quiet she'd relished earlier now loomed large. The next book on the pile was a dog-eared copy of *The Sibley Guide to Birds*; Hugh, she knew, would want that one back. As happened to many couples over the years, Dorie had adopted her husband's interests, convincing herself that she enjoyed bird-watching as much as he did. After they separated, she had joined a local group from her Houston neighborhood, but she hadn't been able to stand listening to Brian Moore with his pedantic expertise and Erica Weston in her galoshes festooned with birds and a matching bag. Besides, Hugh wasn't there to take her hand and half drag her down into the dense black gum, where they would clamber through soggy marshland, ears and eyes alert, breathing hard in exertion and anticipation.

It wasn't until later that she began to distinguish between the parts that were echoes of him and those that reflected her truer self.

The phone rang, and Dorie jumped. "You must be a mind reader," she said dryly after Hugh's greeting.

"What?"

"Oh, nothing," she mumbled.

"How's the move?" His voice sounded thin and far away.

"Fine, although the house painter took forever. He was supposed to be done before I arrived, and he had plenty of time before I moved in."

Hugh was accustomed to her complaints and had learned to treat them like white noise. "It's the holidays, Dorie. I'm surprised he's working at all."

"It's not the holidays; it's the new year already."

"Perhaps you should embrace the slower pace, try to just enjoy being there." The forced patience in his voice both irritated and impressed her, reminding her of what a pain in the ass she could be. If she went much slower, though, she might just stop altogether.

"We missed you at the wedding."

Dorie hadn't expected him to confront her about that. "Did you?" She very much doubted that.

"I'd have liked you there."

"Why?" Her needle voice poked and poked.

"You're family, Dorie."

"We stopped being a family four years ago."

Hugh paused. "We were more than just Harriet once, if you remember."

Just Harriet. Two words that should never be paired together. Just Harriet. Harriet just . . .

Stopped fighting . . .

Needed me to let her go . . .

Harriet just . . . died.

No, she couldn't remember. "You have a new family now."

"We've been through too much together to shut each other out. Sara understands that." His voice was the practiced calm he had perfected after years of listening to unstable patients in his career as a therapist.

"Well, that's very big of her."

Dorie picked up the *Sibley Guide*, as if she could hand it to him then and there, a meager apology for her meanness. "I've been sorting through all my books, and I found your *Sibley*. I set it aside for you." Its pages were marked with sepia coffee-stain rings, Hugh's trademark of a well-loved favorite.

Her own books were filled with miniature scribbles on pages warped from her habit of reading in the bath.

"Oh, that's okay. I replaced that one a while back. You go ahead and keep it."

She thumped it back on top of the pile. The tower tottered and then collapsed, books scattering across the floor.

"Everything okay over there?" Hugh was undoubtedly puzzled by the sudden commotion as Dorie started retrieving the books, the phone clutched between her shoulder and ear.

"Yes!" she barked before collapsing in a heap herself. She reached for Harriet's book, several pages of which had come loose from the binding, and took a deep breath. "I came across Harriet's favorite—remember?"

Hugh paused. "Umm . . ."

"*The Lion, the Witch*—"

"Ah, right. She went through that phase where she was obsessed with wardrobes," Hugh said, his voice like a broken piano string.

Dorie longed to reach him, the real him, and not this recast version he'd constructed. "We read it so many times, it's barely holding together."

Hugh let out a puff of air, and then she heard Sara's voice in the background. "I better let you go," Dorie said. "I've still got lots more unpacking to do."

"Stay in touch, okay?" Hugh said before she hung up.

After the diminutive click of the phone, all she could hear was the distant hum of cars passing the house. Even the waves were silent.

Dorie abandoned the messy pile of books on the floor and went to her desk for Clementine's journal. She decided to just call it a day and go to bed with Clementine's words to keep her company. Picking up the book revealed the dent where she'd impaled Hugh's wedding invitation back at her old house. Dorie ran her finger over it, regretful that she'd spoiled the smooth surface of the wood. A shell she'd found on the beach the day before sat nearby, and she slid it over the scar to hide it.

There. All better.

Dorie took the journal to her bedroom and got ready for bed. Smoothing the covers and plumping the pillows, she settled in, searching for an entry where Clementine talked about Lou again.

September 6, 1999

It's a surreal way to live: not seeing Lou for weeks at a time while he's working on the rigs, and then spending blissful weeks immersed in our world of shared secrets, pasts revealed, and futures planned, all mixed in with hands and tongues and slurred words I blush to think of the morning after. Until he leaves again. It worked for a while, but now the cracks are starting to appear.

Lou talked about opening his own restaurant last night. He said he's going to call it Roustabout because rig work was how he saved enough money to even think about getting it started. It would be home-style Southern cooking, back to basics, comfort food—catfish and grits, gumbo, collard greens, and cornbread. He said we could sell my artwork there. I told him not to dream too big.

I shouldn't have said anything because he started pacing like he always does when he's mad, his anger fracturing the air. I wonder how he kept from burning up like the glowing red embers at the end of his cigarette. He poured another drink, his voice low like he was forcing it down. Then he brought up my parents. He knows not to do that. I told him they had nothing to do with anything. "No shit," he yelled, pacing and pacing. Asshole! He should know better, having a drunk for a father. We got in a huge fight—him throwing things around, me screaming at him. I hate him when he drinks too much.

So I shut him out. Like I always do when anyone tries to get too close. Lou's jobs have started to get closer together, and the gaps between him coming home have grown longer. He sulks because he thinks I don't miss him enough when he's away. I doubt myself and get defensive and shut him out even more. He hurts, drink shading him dark. Last time, I lost track of him for over three months. I forgot to miss him.

Dorie closed the journal and turned off the light. Clementine sounded as if she were difficult to love. Lou too. And a drunk, which complicated things even more. Dorie had always envied Harriet's relationship with her father, their ease together. Neither of them had struggled to show love. Her own restraint had kept her daughter ever so slightly distant, a level of decorum preventing her from displaying the immensity of her love. In fact, the only time Dorie had broken free was when Harriet took her final breath and she had clung to her, clasping the last remnants of life. She hadn't recognized the inhuman sounds that came from her own mouth and hadn't let go of her until Hugh peeled them apart. For a while after Harriet died, it had pained her to look at Hugh and see Harriet in the tilt of his head, in his smile. She would stare long and hard, and Hugh would know why and hadn't been able to bear it.

ferry

Clementine had to be invisible to sneak on and off the boat to the mainland. But it was late. *There are only people half awake, people like me—half alive.* A bellow, like the call of a mammoth sea monster, signaled the ferry's departure, and the engine revved as the boat lurched forward. Droplets of rain glistened on the scruffy paint, where patches of rust bloomed like islands scattered in a pallid sea. The clank of steel reverberated as the wind picked up, whisking away the stink of fish and diesel and car fumes. Steel cranes, salt-worn jetties, and oversized buoys guided them away from the landing dock—replaced by an expanse of turbid sea—*the ferryman delivering me across the River Styx to the world of the dead.* Massive shapes loomed up ahead, crouching low in the water, black and menacing.

Soon, mi corazón. *I will be there very soon.*

housewarming

February 12, 2001

*Y*ou reappeared today, after so long, and I resented the
intrusion. I've spent the last few months learning the
map of Finn's silken whorls cushioning the tender fontanel
that I protect with my palm when I scoop him up to my breast.
I've memorized the folds of his blue-pink petal lids as he
sleeps next to me, his tiny fingers clasping mine. Finn's milky
ambrosia smell has replaced my lover's scent.

What sort of father doesn't meet his own son until he's
already three months old anyway? I insist on feeding Finn
alone in my room for privacy. I make sure he sleeps enough—
more than enough—when Lou is around, shushing Lou
when he laughs too loudly at one of the rig stories he tells to
amuse me. He resents that I don't laugh at his stories anymore, and so he's stopped telling them. And we've stopped
laughing.

First thing the next morning, Dorie sat at the kitchen
table, eating a light breakfast while she read more of Clemen-

tine's journal. No wonder Lou had stopped coming home. Maybe it was better for them both. But for Finn? She wondered which it was who had pushed the other away. Lou seemed afraid to be a father and so had detached himself from their life together. But was Clementine's possessiveness of Finn a result of that or the cause?

Dorie shivered and went to the thermostat to turn up the heat. The temperature inside was sixty degrees—no wonder she was so cold. She fiddled with the controls but couldn't get it to turn on. *Please don't let it be broken. That's all I need.* Her savings were diminishing by the week, and she didn't have enough to cover unexpected expenses like fixing the heat.

She jumped when she heard a knock on the door. Her instinct was to avoid whoever was there by creeping into the bedroom until they left. But Lynn, the blonde from Coconuts, was leaning toward the living room window and holding up what looked like a homemade cake. "Dorie? Morning!"

Dorie reluctantly put down the journal and invited her in. Lynn placed the cake on the kitchen table. "A housewarming gift—made it myself." The smell of blueberries and butter wafted toward them, partially easing Dorie's discomfort over her unexpected visitor.

"Well, this is a surprise." She tried not to sound annoyed.

"Did you get yourself a cat?"

"What? No, she's just a stray that's been hanging around here."

"Well, she's a cutie." Lynn looked around. "Love the place! Rennie told me how nice you'd made it." Dorie was surprised that Rennie would have noticed what the inside of her house looked like enough to comment on it. "He says that too many people build new prefab houses without putting any thought into them. That they all look the same. But he said that yours has . . ."

Lynn paused as if trying to remember his exact words. "Soul. That's what he said."

Dorie wasn't sure how to respond to Rennie commenting on the soulfulness of her house, so she busied herself making a pot of coffee.

"Rennie used to have his own construction business; did he tell you? Was quite particular about what types of houses he built. He even studied architecture for a little bit."

"And now he paints houses?" Dorie asked in surprise.

"Let's sit down and get comfy. Then I can tell you all you want to know about Rennie."

Dorie had to admit, she was intrigued by this new information. They sat down with cups of coffee and plates of cake before Lynn continued.

"We all grew up here together: me, Rennie, and his sister, Shelley. He was always tinkering with stuff, building things, drawing plans. He took off for New Orleans right out of high school, said there was more opportunity there. By the time he met Claire, his business was doing great, and they got married." Lynn took a sip of coffee, and Dorie wondered at this revised version of Rennie. "But he's back home now, left everything behind. Except Carl, their son."

Her impression of Rennie adjusted another fraction, like clicking a knuckle into place. "Why did he come back?"

"Claire cheated on him one too many times. She would always come crawling back to him, and it would work for a bit. But the last time it happened, Rennie decided to stop forgiving her. It's been a while now. Not long enough, though, if you ask me."

"But why didn't he move his business here to the peninsula? Seems like he'd get a lot of work."

"I think he equated his success with Claire, this other life he'd lived. He's happier now, where he belongs. And I think he prefers the slower pace here; we all do."

Perhaps not all of us. Her own internal rhythms had yet to recalibrate to echo those of the surrounding sea and sky.

Lynn ate another bite of cake before getting up and walking around the living room. Dorie had misgivings again about getting rid of the old furnishings, feeling both embarrassed by and protective of the house whose spaces and disorder loomed larger than before Lynn had stepped inside.

"You sure do love to read, huh?" Lynn scanned the bookcase briefly and then picked up Clementine's journal from the couch, opening it to the sketch of Finn. "Who's this? He's a sweetheart. Yours?"

Dorie walked over and took the journal from her, trying not to notice the odd look Lynn gave her. Lynn handed her the sketch, waiting for an explanation.

"It's not mine, actually." Lynn continued to watch her, obviously curious. "I found it in some boxes in the garage when I moved in."

Lynn's eyes widened. "So whose is it, then?"

"It seems to have belonged to a woman who used to live here." Part of her wanted to keep Clementine to herself, but another part wondered if Lynn could shed any light on what had happened to her. "Clementine del Castillo. Do you know her?"

"Hmm, rings a bell, I think. Not sure, though. I thought I knew most people around here, but she must have kept a very low profile. Who's the boy?" Lynn gestured to the drawing Dorie still held in her hand.

"Her son, I think."

"So what's happened to them? Where are they now?"

"I don't know."

Lynn looked at Dorie as if assessing her involvement with Clementine's story. "What about the father?"

"I think he's in prison."

"Really? The plot thickens! What did he do?"

Dorie shrugged, resisting the urge to make excuses for him, as if she knew anything at all, really. She prickled with frustration at all Lynn's questions—the same questions she had and couldn't answer.

Lynn held up a finger. "Wait a minute! I think I do know who she is. I heard about a resident whose son drowned last year sometime."

Dorie's stomach clenched, and she looked down at the smiling boy in the drawing. Another child gone. Another mother recast.

"That must be him." Lynn moved closer to Dorie so she could see the boy again. They both stood quietly, side by side, Dorie trying to swallow down the lump in her throat.

"I heard she disappeared," Dorie said. "No one seems to know what happened to her."

Lynn looked up at Dorie. "And now here you are, living in her house. Odd, isn't it?"

Dorie sensed fate intervening—a thick black cord threading through her and Clementine's worlds, intersecting, twisting, searching until it found them and bound them together.

Lynn turned and picked up her purse. "Shoot, I've got to go. I've got a plumber coming soon to look at one of the cottages. Here's my number. Call me if you need anything or just want to hang out."

Dorie walked her to the door. "Thanks for the housewarming gift."

"You're welcome!" Lynn's voice held a brightness that scraped against Dorie's skin, grazing the surface layer.

As soon as Dorie had closed the door, she went to the kitchen table and opened her computer. When she searched *Clementine del Castillo*, there were a couple of entries related to her artwork and local shows she'd been in, but nothing very recent. So she began searching for news stories of local drownings. Eventually, she found one that seemed to fit the dates and descriptions of Clementine and her son.

Child Drowns at San Luis Pass
Wednesday, July 14, 2004

A four-year-old boy drowned on Monday. "The local boy and his mother were picnicking on the beach under the San Luis Pass Bridge, which connects Brazoria and Galveston counties," said Brazoria County Sheriff's Office investigator Mike Stoltz.

Around 2:55 p.m., the boy asked his mother for a fishing net. She handed it to him and turned back to a painting she was working on. When she looked up, the child was gone.

Dorie's eyes blurred with tears, the familiar shadow of despair threatening. *He died in July, only two months before I first saw the yellow house. My god—he's only been dead a few months.* She wiped the tears away with her sleeve and looked back at the computer screen.

"He must have lost his balance and been carried away by the undertow," Stoltz said. Stoltz urged both adults and children in the area to always wear life jackets around the water.

"Don't take any chances," he said. "We've got a mom now without her baby."

Dorie reached for the sketch of the boy. *They must have sat at this very table, Clementine watching him eat as she captured his enthusiasm with graphite lines on pale paper. Did she continue to draw him after he died, summoning him from memory as she sat here alone while the waves murmured below?*

Clementine's rendering of Finn—all that was left of him now—smiled back at Dorie.

san luis pass, galveston

Clementine forced her legs to lift and step, to move closer to where she had lost him. It had taken days to get there. *How can it look the same? How can it not ooze decay and filth for what it did to my boy?* She pressed her hands hard against her eyes to force away the image of his blue face when they'd pulled him from the water that day.

Searching the brine-soaked jetty for some sign that he was there, she found a sharp sea stone and pressed it into the soft black wood to mark his name. Clementine stepped to the icy edge and listened for him in the waves. She cursed this dark water, this trickster that deceived with its gentle current that could turn vicious, covetous.

She collected sea rocks—only the smoothest—and stacked them. Mixed in shells and a feather for good measure—*a cairn to mark his place*. She waited for him through the long night.

And when the sun burned the horizon, she knew he wasn't there.

like a mermaid

June 15, 2002

Lou's been showing up sporadically, trying to work his way back into our lives while also seeming to slowly disappear, piece by piece. Finn fell yesterday and scraped his knee. When Lou tried to comfort him, he cried even louder, until I had to take him from Lou's arms. It's as if I live on one side of the mirror and Lou on the other—the same room, but not. He's only staying until tomorrow this time, and we've barely spoken. But I can see that he's heartbroken. We just don't know how to fix it.

Dorie brought down a bowl of milk for the cat before heading to the beach. It was curled up in a spot of sunlight, next to a clump of rosemary that looked like it had been part of an herb garden at one point.

I wonder if Clementine planted it.

The cat jumped up, rubbing against Dorie's legs and purring. "Now, now, it's only a bit of milk." She couldn't help but

51

linger for a second to watch it lap at the bowl, the milk sprinkling its face. She chuckled to herself.

Scattered driftwood and carelessly discarded plastic bottles punctuated the endless stretch of shoreline. Dorie increased her pace, her body loosening and her lungs opening to the sea air.

Then she spotted her neighbor up ahead. "Morning, Curtis." It was good to see a familiar face—always tanned. His hands fidgeted, as if adjusting his line even when he wasn't fishing, readying the reel for his next catch.

"Mornin'." He raised his rod in greeting, the handle tucked close against the side of his belly like a beloved pet.

"Caught anything worthwhile?" she asked as she got closer.

"Yep. Got me a shark—little 'un, but tasty, I bet." He gestured to a cooler on the sand behind him. Dorie approached it to peek inside, remembering Clementine's journal entry: *a thread of red trailed its feeble attempts to escape, tethering it to its fate.*

She stuffed her hands into her pockets and rubbed a smooth rock she'd picked up the day before, a treasure she'd forgotten she had. "Do you remember a woman called Clementine? I think maybe she used to live in my house."

"Sure," said Curtis, staring out at the sea. Dorie held her breath, not wanting to miss anything Curtis had to say about Clementine. After a moment of silence, he continued. "She was a beauty—long dark hair in waves. Like a mermaid, Leanne always said." He pulled the line taut and wound the reel, taking a few steps deeper into the water.

"What happened to her?" Dorie asked, longing to know more, hoping he knew where she was.

"Some say she went back to her family in Mexico. Others, that she joined her boy in the sea."

Dorie squeezed the rock tighter in her hand. "What do you mean?"

"Ah, you know how people are . . . making up stories."

Curtis pulled in his line, bit by bit, coaxing the fish closer to him. Then he stilled, waiting patiently for his catch to wear itself out before reeling it all the way in.

"Finn was only a scrap, barely out of diapers. They used to spend hours on the beach together, looking for shells, drawing, just horsing around. She didn't look much more than a kid herself, and raising him all on her own. Well, for the most part. I'd see a guy around every once in a while."

Lou.

"When did you last see her?"

"Missus went by around the fall this past year, and the place was empty."

Dorie's skin prickled like a hot rash spreading. So when she had first found her yellow house, Clementine must have abandoned it just weeks before.

"We tried to offer her a hand after he passed, being on her own and all. The wife took her some casseroles; I gave her some of my catch a few times. Always took it without a word, just a nod. Never was a real sociable sort. Checked the house a few more times, but she just up and left—everything still in the house. When I checked with Beachcomber's, who took care of the property, no one there knew where she'd gone. Apparently, she'd quit paying the rent for a couple of months, so they weren't too bothered by her leaving."

"No one tried looking for her?"

Curtis's shoulders rose and fell, his rod moving in unison with them. "Well, you might try asking Agnes and Earle; they live down a ways." Curtis gestured with his head back toward the road. "Beauchamp Ranch. You can't miss it." Dorie vaguely remembered a large rusty sign looming over herds of cows that looked oddly incongruous living just across from the ocean. "Clementine used to work for them; they might have found out something. They sure did worry when she left."

He paused again, muttering, and moved farther into the water, recasting his line. His voice caught between the folds of waves.

Dorie needed to keep walking, fast and hard. She raised her hand in farewell, but Curtis was already wading even deeper, absorbed in the immensity of the ocean surrounding him. She recalled the sighting she'd had a couple of weeks ago when she first moved in—the green lights, the yin-yang symbol in the sand, the reopening of her own wounds. There was a Mexican legend she'd taught years ago: La Llorona. She was a mother who had drowned her children in revenge against her husband, and then had drowned herself in remorse. She was said to haunt the water, wailing for her lost children.

Dorie shivered, despite the muggy air. To lose Finn so suddenly like that, without warning.

Even though she and Hugh had known for years that Harriet was so sick they might lose her, the knowing and the reality of loss were vastly different. The sudden emptiness of their home had been filled temporarily with visitors and funeral plans, a distraction from their grief. They had had to select music, readings, a special dress for Harriet. White laced with pink ribbon. No one should be buried in a dress so small. It had been like planning a wedding, something she would never do for her daughter now.

But the overwhelming yet essential set of tasks had forced her to stay afloat, to put Harriet's needs before her own one last time. She had wanted to properly honor her daughter's memory.

At the funeral home, the funeral director had given them a tour of caskets set out like fine automobiles in a showroom: shiny and slick, trimmed with gleaming metal. The casket he had recommended was immensely large. The director had apologized profusely when Hugh told him that Harriet was only eight years old. He'd then proceeded to show them a tiny white coffin with pink satin lining—perfect for a daughter lost too soon.

When Dorie reached the house, the cat scampered up the steps and began brushing against her legs. She reached down to stroke its head, and it looked up at her with such trust.

"Okay, I think it's time to give you a good bath." She'd have to get some flea shampoo to clean her up properly. "Now, what shall we call you?"

the strand, galveston

Clementine watched the waxing of the moon each night, waiting for it to be a sliver away from whole. Then she would journey home to find her lost boy. But for now, she had to keep walking these streets, counting the red bricks, worn through the ages. When the night was dark and she didn't have to see. Mesmerized by the shiny bits in between, tracks she followed to nowhere. Cold through the sole of her broken shoe.

She traveled far through a maze of buildings too high to look at, ghost impressions covering their walls. And people who stared like they knew. Who moved away to the edge of the bricks, who saw sadness oozing from her like pus from a sore.

I am Lazarus, brought back from the grave. Or perhaps I am the other Lazarus, the beggar rewarded upon his death to watch the fortunate suffer—those mothers who haven't lost their babies.

mingling

March 26, 2003

t he beach was crowded today; rows of trucks lined the water, the waves retreating from them silently, drowned out by the squeals and shouts from the tumult of spring breakers who invade each year. But Finn insisted on spending time by the water, so we went extra early to avoid the masses.

A little boy about Finn's age came over and started helping him dig a hole in the sand. I left them to it and disappeared into my sketchbook and music, the latter a soundtrack that directed my hand's movements. They ended up playing all morning. I don't think I've ever seen Finn play with another child before. My solitude shouldn't be something he's forced to share.

Later, I felt guilty because he got a sunburn. He has his father's skin, not mine.

Dorie closed the journal, her hand lingering on the cover as if holding the words still. Harriet, like Finn, had lacked friends. She'd been sick for so much of her short life that socializing with her peers had never been much of a priority. She had known some kids at MD Anderson, and they had spent time together at the hospital. But it had been rare for her to have a playdate.

"Why don't I have any friends, Mom?" she'd asked Dorie one day.

"You do have friends. You have Daisy and dad and me. Your cousins."

"That's not really the same."

Kids had known she was different, had been afraid of her fragility. Dorie had homeschooled her because Harriet couldn't consistently keep up with her studies. So Harriet had never experienced the thrill of a best friend and the heartache of losing one.

And Clementine's solitude had meant losing the man she once loved. Dorie herself had done the same. *I mustn't retreat again; I must make more of an effort.*

Bob's was a hole-in-the-wall bar in the middle of the peninsula, famous for the life-sized figures of the Blues Brothers that greeted customers as they entered and the homey vibe that attracted locals and tourists alike. She and Hugh used to go there quite often years ago. The last time they'd gone, they'd sung along to an eighties cover band, grinning sheepishly and feeling young again.

It was Tuesday today. Surely it wouldn't be crowded on a Tuesday.

Dorie could hear the noise as she approached the door and had to fight the urge to turn around and get back in her car. *Come on, Dorie, you can do it. Just grab a bite to eat and a drink. No big deal.*

Tonight's performer was a man in his early twenties, his guitar like an extra appendage. Duct tape covered a hole in the instrument's scuffed-up body. Shaggy blond hair occasionally revealed eyes that played with his audience, who were obviously charmed.

Several people cried out requests for "Margaritaville," an obvious crowd favorite. He teased them with another song that Dorie didn't recognize, and most of the audience sat down. But when he hit the last note, he grinned widely, paused amid the muffled anticipation of the room, and then struck those familiar opening chords. The audience immediately let out whoops and yeehaws, and almost half of them got to their feet, thrilled he'd fulfilled their request.

A sunburned, potbellied man started jigging about, almost losing his balance and bumping into Dorie's table. "Sorry, ma'am," he slurred before stumbling toward the stage, arms waving in the air, singing loudly. The audience lost itself in the song as the young man maneuvered the stage with ease.

He shone!

Dorie felt a light touch on her shoulder and looked up to see Rennie smiling down at her. He looked different somehow—perhaps only because he wasn't in his work clothes.

"Want to join me for a drink?" he asked loudly over the din. She hadn't expected to see anyone she knew tonight, but the music had stirred her up, and she was pleased to see a familiar face. "Let's go outside—too noisy in here." He gestured to the deck out back.

Dorie stood and followed him through the doors. The night held onto the warmth of the day, and the moon shone full and bright. A barge lumbered by through the dark water as they sat at a table and ordered drinks. The song drew to an end in the next room, followed by high-pitched squeals and lusty off-key roars from the crowd.

"He's very popular," she said, gesturing inside.

"Especially when he sings the old favorites. The number of times he has to sing 'Margaritaville,' I'm surprised he still does it. The first time, he ended up making so much in tips, it was well worth it. Then it sort of became his regular opener. Course, he'd rather sing his own songs."

"You sound like a fan."

"His biggest." Rennie smiled and then looked toward the doors leading inside. "Speak of the devil . . ."

"Hey, Dad. Enjoying the show?"

The young performer stood before them, his hand resting on Rennie's shoulder. Dorie remembered Lynn mentioning that Rennie had a son. He had his father's eyes, blue as water in sunlight and shining, and suddenly she wanted to understand them both better.

"We just came outside for a bit of air. Hey, this here is Dorie. She's new to the peninsula. Dorie, my son, Carl."

Carl had a disarming openness to his face, as though he wasn't afraid of life. "Nice to meet you." He sat down and pulled out a cigarette. "You mind?" Dorie shook her head.

Rennie patted him on the back. "That new song you did was good Carl. Real good."

"Well, I think you may be the only one here who'd agree, Dad."

Dorie spoke up. "I agree." She noticed a gaggle of young girls twittering just by the doors to the deck, whispering and eyeing Carl from afar. They looked like they wouldn't be able to restrain themselves for much longer. "And so do they, by the look of it." She gestured to the doors.

Carl followed her gaze and then smiled back at her. Then he turned his attention to Rennie. Watching the two of them interact lifted Dorie's spirits, and she was glad to be there in that din. They both had a confidence and ease about them, but where Rennie's was stiller and quieter, Carl expressed his outwardly, sharing himself with the world.

"Hey, I got a gig in Austin. I'm leaving next week." Carl tapped his hand on the table to the music.

"That's great news," Rennie said, though his eyes betrayed some worry. "You staying with Tracey?"

Carl shrugged. "Not sure yet. I've got to talk to her." He looked over at the girls waiting for him. "Hey, I'll see you later. Don't wait up." His face immediately transformed as he eased up from the table and sauntered over to the girls, wearing a lopsided grin. He was the star again. Carl put his arm around a tiny brunette, who practically hopped in place with excitement. The others fell back in deference to her, their shoulders sagging a little.

Rennie messed with the label of his longneck. "So, that's Carl." He looked up at Dorie, and she tried to ignore the sudden flutter in her stomach. They listened to the next song for a bit before he continued. "He wants to leave, try his hand at being a bona fide musician, broaden his horizons. Course, I support it, but that's an awful big dream to follow."

"Following dreams can be a tricky business," Dorie said, wondering whether she should bring up Rennie's past. "But he's young. He has plenty of time to figure things out. It gets harder to do when you're older."

"I suppose, although it's never too late. You just have to listen to yourself, figure out what makes you happy."

"Like being a house painter?"

"Sure. Why not?" He laughed, and Dorie wanted to laugh with him. "And are you doing what makes you happy?"

If only he knew how she'd been spending her time since moving there, obsessively devouring the life of a stranger, a woman who'd lost everything. "Well, I moved here, didn't I?"

Rennie looked at her quizzically, as if he knew there was more to it than that. "And what are you going to do with yourself now that you're here?"

She fidgeted, glancing at her purse. "I haven't quite figured that out yet." Taking a large gulp of her margarita, she grimaced as the pain of brain freeze shot through her head.

"You okay?" Rennie asked.

Dorie nodded. "So, did owning your own business not make you happy?"

"You been talking to Lynn?" Rennie's question had Dorie shifting in her seat. "That was a long time ago. I like things less complicated these days." Dorie supposed being married to Claire must have been pretty complicated, based on what Lynn had told her. Rennie took another drink. "So what did you do before? In Houston?"

"Some editing work. Before that, I was a teacher." A pinch on her arm alerted her to a mosquito, and she slapped it into a red smear.

"Why did you stop teaching?"

Dorie scratched at the bump growing on her forearm and recalled the shame she'd felt when the school had asked her to go on sabbatical. She'd eventually turned in her notice after months of them asking when she was coming back.

"I don't know. Just needed a change."

"Think you'll ever go back to it?"

"Never say never." She shrugged, attempting a light-hearted smile.

"Hey, my niece, Izzie, has been having a hard time in school. Maybe you could help her out some. Shel can't spend the time with her that she needs, and they're getting on each other's last nerve."

Dorie shivered as a cool breeze blew in from the water. "Perhaps."

"Shel's on a budget, so I'm not sure we can afford you," he teased, his eyes crinkling. "But between the two of us, we could hopefully make it worth your while."

That would certainly contribute to solving her money problems, especially if she had to replace the heating system.

Rennie smiled Carl's lopsided grin. "We sure would appreciate it."

"I'll let you know," Dorie said, trying to force away the memory of weeping before stacks of essays, her tears blurring loops of blue ink that rendered tales of broken friendships and fractured families. She'd stopped teaching when Harriet's doctor appointments took over. When her only purpose was to keep her daughter alive. Later, after they'd lost her, she had tried to go back. But she had been forced still at the classroom door by packs of schoolgirls in the hallways giggling over their latest crushes. By boys thickening the stale air with their silent adolescent angst. All until she could not go back anymore.

Dorie fumbled with her purse and put a twenty on the table. "Well, I think it's time for me to get going. I really didn't plan to stay out so late tonight."

Rennie stood when she did. "You sure you don't want another drink?"

"No, thanks." She began pushing her way through the mad crowd of squealing girls and sweaty men bellowing along with Carl at the top of their inebriated lungs.

This mingling business was harder than she'd hoped.

downtown alleyways, galveston

*S*trangers passed Clementine on the street, their complacency a punch in the gut. *Don't look into their faces. I don't want to see the me they see.*

She found an alleyway filled with the stink of trash and piss. She picked up a half-eaten sandwich tossed next to the dumpster. *No matter. I can't taste it anyway.*

At first, it was easier to find a place to sleep that wasn't the red bricks. But they didn't look at her anymore, those men with stares like tar—that was when she knew she had a place to lay her head. Now it was only men who wandered the streets.

Only they will have me now, will share their pallets of sticky clothes, their precious sips that dull what I let them do to me later—while I stare at the stars shining above me. Sometimes, I'm lucky and don't even remember.

absence

May 31, 2004

> *I lost my temper with Finn today. He broke a vase in a house I was cleaning. He looked so shocked when he broke it, eyes wide as I hurled my frustration and desperation at him. His remorse fueled my anger, so I felt vindicated when dismissing his apology. He reminded me so much of his father, I couldn't bear to look at him and see his need for my mercy, like a prayer.*
>
> *I have to be stronger so he can grow to be a better man than his father. A better person than each of his parents.*

Dorie reread the last line. *How good a parent was I? Not good enough. Never good enough. Of course, frustration and fear manifest in anger. Most people regret not being more patient with their children.*

She had taken her own anger out on Hugh most often, rather than Harriet. She'd used her stone face on him countless times. But Harriet had experienced it too, without Dorie realizing it. Harriet had once told her that when Dorie had her mad face on, Harriet wanted to melt into a big puddle like a snowman.

Dorie had hated herself for that. And Clementine had only had Finn at which to direct her anger. No one else.

Dorie had lost her temper with the cat earlier that day because she'd been scratching on the new sofa, so she'd shooed Rosie out of the house. She'd decided on that name because of the cat's preferred napping spot next to the rosemary bush. Dorie went to the front door now and called to Rosie, needing to assure her that the cat was wanted. Rosie scampered up the steps to the deck. She brushed against Dorie's legs, releasing her rosemary scent into the air.

Was it at Beauchamp Ranch that Finn broke the vase? Perhaps they would know what had happened to Clementine. It was time to pay them a visit.

Dorie parked on the dirt track leading to the entrance of Beauchamp Ranch. Curtis hadn't given her a number to call ahead, and she worried about how welcoming they'd be to a stranger. But her will to know more about Clementine emboldened her.

As she walked down the driveway, chickens scattered in a panic, squawking indignantly. Their feathers were a dazzling white, just like the house up ahead, which looked freshly painted. Three toffee-colored cows stared stoically at her over a barbed-wire fence, making her strangely self-conscious. All the windows were so clean, she could see straight into the front room, the pale interior walls winking back at her as the sun caught the glass.

A quiet buzzing like an insect chorus announced the approach of an elderly woman with a mass of white hair like a swarm of barely visible gnats flying about her head. Her arthritic fingers clasped the control of her electric wheelchair awkwardly, like a young child holding a pencil. When she stopped abruptly before Dorie, the chickens settled down nearby and clucked gently, their comical voices lending an absurd levity to Dorie's anxiety as she struggled to introduce herself.

"I'm Dorie," she said. The woman looked at her silently, her face framed by the bright whiteness of her hair. "Curtis is my neighbor. He said you might know . . ." Dorie struggled to broach the subject, hoping that maybe Curtis had mentioned she might stop by. "I'm sorry to just show up like this, but he said you knew Clementine del Castillo." Her words ran into each other, and she wondered if the woman even understood her.

The woman stretched her neck forward just a fraction, fixing her eyes on Dorie. "You know where she is?"

"I was hoping perhaps you did." Dorie's voice was low, deflated by the prospect of another dead end. She realized that she'd half expected Clementine to be here, safe and looked after.

"You better come on in." The woman pulled on the controls of her wheelchair so she glided like a fish through water. "My name's Agnes, by the way." Dorie trailed behind her, up the ramp and into the house, her shoes too loud on the wooden boards.

Agnes led her into the front room, where Dorie sat on an old velvet sofa that sagged in the middle, leaving her lopsided. "What's your interest in Clementine?"

Dorie wrung her hands as she provided a rote answer of wanting to return some of Clementine's things, not sure herself of the real explanation.

Agnes looked at her skeptically. "Clementine helped me with the housework. Came every week with her son, Finn."

She paused, looking up at a cross above the fireplace, her gaze lingering, her lips moving without speaking. Hammering from outside disturbed the dust motes that glinted in the shards of sunlight slanting through gaps in the partially drawn curtains, turning the room a gauzy gold. "Earle used to spend time with the boy while Clementine worked. The boy helped him feed the animals and loved the chickens."

Dorie smiled, longing for more. She tried to conjure a living form from the sketch in Clementine's journal, almost forgetting he'd been a real boy.

Agnes's eyes glazed over as she looked out the window into the yard. "One time, when we'd fixed one of them up for supper, Finn asked where Goldie was. Earle told him she'd run away and snuck onto a boat, where she sailed the seas with pirates, laying eggs to pay her passage. He liked that story, made Earle tell it over and over."

"Where did Clementine go?" asked Dorie.

"We took her in for a bit, after Finn died."

Agnes looked at the worn velvet sofa where Dorie sat, and Dorie felt Clementine there, laying under a blanket, removing herself from the world—a waif, barely real, pale and translucent, like the ocean early in the morning when the light shines it silver.

"Earle went over to the house and made her come back with him." Agnes reached over to the table next to her, her veined hand rubbing the worn leather of an old Bible. "Then a few months later, she was gone. Picked up and left in the night." Agnes picked up the Bible and put it in her lap.

"When was this?" asked Dorie.

"Beginning of this year—wasn't a good time for any of us."

Clementine had been right here when Dorie moved into the yellow house. "And you have no idea where she is now?"

"We tried searching for her, of course. Even went into Galveston, asked around at a few churches and homeless shelters. She'd been there, but we weren't able to find her. Earle even tried talking to the police, but they were no help. Said they'd let us know if they found anything."

Dorie heard the hammering stop, followed by heavy booted steps clomping across the wooden back porch. Agnes lowered her voice. "She doesn't want to be found. Not by us, anyway."

The creak of the screen door opening and then clicking shut announced the arrival of a burly elderly man. His heft was diminished by his contained movements and lowered gaze. Agnes raised her voice again, as if to adjust the tension in the room. "Earle, come on over here and meet Dorie."

Earle removed his cowboy hat and raised his eyes. "Afternoon." Agnes looked up at him and asked how it was going with the porch. "Fine. Should be done by the time they all arrive."

Agnes turned back to Dorie and explained that her husband was building out the back porch, screening it in for the grandkids so they could put in some bunk beds. "Our brood is growing by the minute, and they sure do love to come visit." She moved over to a nearby table and picked up a photo in a large silver frame, her tone becoming more congenial as she talked about her family. "This was taken last summer out back, next to the live oak. Dan Jr. wanted to swing on the tire Earle had attached to it, and he fought staying still long enough to take this photo."

"Agnes bribed him with her homemade chocolate praline so he'd stand still and smile with his sisters," said Earle, looking at his wife fondly.

"He rushed off as soon as the photo was taken, flying high into the branches, gripping the rope and squealing and hollering. I'm always afraid he's going to fall and break his arm." Agnes slowly shook her head and tutted.

Earle walked toward the kitchen, where Dorie heard him opening the fridge and pouring liquid into a glass. Agnes moved her chair in his direction. "Earle, we've got a visitor, for heaven's sake! How about sharing some of that lemonade!" She joined him in the kitchen, where cupboards were opened and glasses clinked and then lowered voices whispered.

Dorie looked around the room, noticing the detailed woodwork of the moldings and a carved fireplace mantle that showed a rare level of workmanship. There was a collection of black-and-white photos on one wall displaying a young woman on horseback who resembled Agnes. One showed her standing next to the same horse, her hand on its neck, and in another, she was smiling wide and holding a large trophy.

Agnes and Earle reentered the room minutes later, Earle bearing a tray laden with a jug of lemonade and glasses. Dorie imagined Agnes rising from the wheelchair and striding toward her, a bold smile across her face. Earle set down the tray and poured Dorie a drink.

"You have a beautiful home."

"Why, thank you. Earle built this place with his own two hands." Agnes looked at Earle with pride. "We've been here going on fifty years now, isn't that right, Earle?" Earle nodded and handed her a glass of lemonade, already beaded from the ice. "We'll leave it to the kids so they can enjoy it after we're gone. They're settled in Houston right now. Our son teaches at TSU, so it'll be a while before they think about living here full-time. But it'll happen." Agnes looked again at the photo that sat among a tabletop full of other family members.

"You must have seen lots of changes over the years," Dorie said, taking a sip of the tart lemonade that made her lips pucker.

"Sure have. I expect there's lots more to come. Seems the real world is starting to catch up with us finally. But we're tucked away back here at the ranch, so it doesn't bother us too much. Right Earle?"

Earle seemed lost in thought, perhaps back in the past when things were simpler. *When the people he cared about were still whole,* thought Dorie.

"Earle!" Agnes called, raising her voice to get his attention. He dragged himself back to them and nodded, then took a swallow of lemonade.

Dorie longed to mine Agnes for more details, to go back to the Clementine and Finn before she lost him. But Dorie sensed they weren't a topic Earle was comfortable talking about.

"Well, I won't keep you." She stood. The air in the room felt heavy with both age and absence.

Agnes accompanied her to the door, and Dorie asked her to please let her know if Clementine turned up. Agnes looked into the living room to make sure Earle couldn't overhear.

"She will. The Lord will guide her back to us. I'm certain of that."

rot

Clementine dreamed of her father again. His pressed black suit, hands clasped in front, eyes empty. He handed her a mango, heavy and ripe, from their orchard near Monterrey. She held it to her nose, inhaling the scent, pungent like forbidden fruit.

"Why are *you* here and not her?" he asked in a voice hollow and flat.

The fruit began to soften and rot in Clementine's hand, until she smelled her dead mother's breath as she kissed her cheek, like so long ago.

"*Su madre*, she gave her life for you. And you throw yours away, *como si no fuese nada.*"

Clementine dropped the rotted fruit with a thud and a splat.

"Shame on you—*debería darle verguenza.*"

Flies, buzzing and frenzied, circled in a black cloud of gluttony that rose and enveloped her.

Until she disappeared.

unravel

orie awoke with a start, gulping for breath. Clementine's journal dug into her side where she had left it when she finally fell asleep. Rosie tensed and then stood, annoyed at being woken so abruptly. During the long night, Dorie had slept intermittently, plagued by nightmares of wandering the dunes with Clementine in her search of their lost children. Of drowning in a dark sea.

Fingers of early light reached through the curtains and dragged her back to reality. She reached for the journal, the pages flipping so quickly that Clementine's handwriting shifted like a moving image, delicate loops morphing into a scribbled web of barely legible lines. Last night, she'd struggled to make out the final words on the last page, which were accompanied by a swirl of ink scrawled so intensely that the pen had ripped through the paper.

Please take me too. I am done.

Sorrow tugged at Dorie's dark edges, threatening to unravel them and burrow inside to reach the tiny black speck she'd buried so deep. Perhaps Clementine had visited the water so she wouldn't forget. People thought that when someone died, their loved ones tried to forget and move forward, to avoid the pain of loss. But that wasn't true. It was the fear of forgetting that weighed on her. The panic, when she couldn't remember the exact color of that fleck in Harriet's iris, the way her top lip curved slightly higher on the left than the right when she smiled, her little-girl scent, like summer rain.

Dorie picked up the phone and dialed. "Hey—I need to see you. Today."

Hugh paused. "Are you in town?"

"No. But I can get there in an hour."

"What's wrong?"

A cloud moved across the weak morning sun, and shadows cupped the small bedroom in their hands.

Hugh sighed. "You better come, then."

Dorie made sure there was enough food and water for Rosie, glad she'd had Rennie install a cat door so Rosie could come and go as she liked. Dorie wondered if Rosie would still be there when she returned.

She closed up the house, hopeful that the new locks would keep Lou out.

Dorie stopped for gas in Winnie, a typical small Texas community with traffic signals swaying over a single-lane road, next to a two-pump gas station, a mom-and-pop grocery, and a Waffle House. She started to fill up her car as she sipped acrid coffee from a foam cup, her hand shaking slightly. She prayed that Sara and her daughter wouldn't be at the house when she arrived.

It was still a struggle sometimes not to think of Hugh as hers. He and Sara had met when they were both birding in

Anahuac. After Dorie had refused to go with him anymore. After she'd become still and silent, locked inside the fading montage of their daughter's too-short life.

Hugh had stumbled down a steep, shaggy dune and found Sara alternately scribbling in a notebook and tilting her head back to search the sky for birds. Regal, Hugh had told Dorie. Their mutual attraction had been immediate, but he said they'd refused to acknowledge it for several more months. The relationship had hovered precariously between friendship and love, until Dorie recovered enough for him to tell her about Sara.

She didn't know why he had felt the need to share those details with her. Perhaps a sense of intimacy and trust that he had wanted to maintain, or a way to assuage his guilt at finding love again without her. A way to include her.

The click of the gas pump pulled Dorie back to the now-lukewarm coffee in her hand and the commuters readying for their return to the city. She tossed her cup in the trash before starting up the car and putting on the radio to fill the silence.

Soon after she pulled onto the busy highway, a heavy rain began to beat against the car window. The world blurred, forcing her to focus only on the brake lights ahead of her to keep from swerving into traffic. Everything else was rinsed into an abstract watercolor landscape of limpid greens and blues and grays. She and a few other drivers pulled onto the narrow shoulder, drowning in waves that surged out from the enormous semis speeding by, undeterred by the torrential downpour.

Once the rain had dissipated, Dorie continued driving along the freeway until she reached Houston. There, she began navigating busy intersections, strip malls, and pissed-off commuters. By the time she pulled into Hugh's driveway, she was vibrating with a harried, frenetic energy, and she gripped the steering wheel to still herself. When she rang the doorbell, a dog barked, and its clicking footsteps grew louder as it reached the door.

"Chester, hush." Through the window, she saw Hugh grip the dog's collar before opening the front door.

Dorie sat on the couch, her hands clasped tightly in her lap. On the table next to her was a silver-framed photograph of two girls dressed formally in white organza, wreaths of flowers adorning their hair. One was whispering into the other's ear, her cupped hand obscuring most of the listener's face, which appeared intent on their shared secret. Dorie supposed one of them was probably Sara's daughter, Ruby—a flower girl at their wedding.

"Is Sara here?" she asked.

Hugh went to sit in a nearby armchair. "No, she's at the store."

"I want to see the album."

Hugh sighed heavily and went to the bookshelf to pull it from its place. Dorie kept only one photo of Harriet. For months after she died, Dorie had poured over photos, videos, hours of footage. And then she had stopped. It was impossible to reconcile the Harriet in the videos and photographs with the one who had spent her last months straddling this world and the next. Her memory of Harriet's face had started to falter, replaced by images captured with a lens. Looking at photos of Harriet was a painful reminder that she continued to slowly fade from their lives, even now.

Dorie and Hugh sat side by side and opened the well-worn pages:

Harriet as a baby, asleep, propped against the crib railings, surrounded by open board books, dreaming of the red balloon in the great green room.

On the next page, Harriet beamed back at them. Her first day of school. Her uniform was drab, but somehow she glowed, her brave smile the only hint of unease.

Turning the page . . .

Harriet held out her peanut butter sandwich for Daisy, who reached for it tentatively with her black puppy snout. Knowing she wasn't usually allowed to eat from Harriet's hand, yet knowing she wouldn't get in trouble *this* time.

Dorie's tears blurred the images as they reached the last page.

Harriet safe in Uncle Felix's arms at his wedding, bleary eyed with exhaustion but still trying to look pretty for the camera. Her yellow silk dress creased, her hair loosened from its ribbons.

Hugh closed the album with a solemn finality. "What brought this on, Dorie?"

"What do you mean?"

"The phone call, this visit, the album?"

She leaned away from him. When he talked to her as the therapist he was, rational and detached, the space between them grew until she forgot how it felt to love him. Right after Harriet died, they'd clung to one another and cried endlessly. But then Dorie became pale and silent, locked inside herself for months.

At first, he'd tried everything to reach her: Forcing her to talk about her feelings, which led mostly to slammed doors and the bitter aftertaste of recrimination. Trying to give her space to grieve, which only allowed in a deeper and irretrievable silence that lasted for days. She'd taken antidepressants for a while, mostly just to stop from constantly crying. But that had made it even easier for her to withdraw. He invited friends and family over, whom she mostly ignored and thereby alienated indefinitely. Then he tried to offer her an overabundance of affection, the result of which finally convinced him he'd lost her.

"Something must have triggered this," Hugh said, digging further.

"I found a journal when I moved into the house. Of a woman who used to live there."

"A journal?"

"I think she's suicidal." *Unless it's already too late.*

"For God's sake, Dorie." Hugh stood up abruptly. "It's someone else's life, not yours. You have to distance yourself from this; it's not good for you."

"Good for me?"

He looked at her, concern creasing his face. "You can't fix any of it."

"It's not about fixing anything." She looked away, hating that he knew her so well. Hugh hadn't been able to fix their marriage any more than she had. His coping mechanism had been Sara. He'd been so relieved that Dorie wouldn't fight the separation. In fact, she'd wanted it as much as he had, although for different reasons. Hugh had been ready to move forward, start over. She had just wanted to be alone so she wouldn't have to love anyone anymore.

Hugh's voice softened. "Look, I just worry about you out there by yourself, immersed in these morose thoughts. It's not healthy."

The distance was expanding, between where Dorie still sat on the sofa and where Hugh stood next to the bookcase. She tried again to pull him back in, closer to her. "I've met some people." She pictured Lynn and Rennie joking with each other, her arm linked through his, rings catching the light.

"Good." Hugh turned his back to her and replaced Harriet's album on the shelf where it belonged. She visualized the box hidden in the attic of the yellow house, *Harriet* written on the side in black permanent marker. Filled with horse drawings that had plastered the walls of her old room, stuffed animals that had crowded her pink bed—those pieces of Harriet that had been embedded in the old house and were now shut up in a box.

At that moment, the back door opened, and Sara called out, "Hello, we're home," as if giving them a moment to compose themselves before entering the scene. She'd obviously been forewarned that Dorie would be there and in a state.

Two girls entered the living room, followed by the dog, whose bounding excitement was obviously annoying one of them immensely. "God, Mom! Is he ever going to grow out of this?"

"Chester, come here!" The dog sat obediently next to Sara. "Ruby, say hello to Mrs. Edwards." She faltered slightly at having to introduce Dorie with the same surname, which they now all shared. Dorie decided it was probably time to change back to her maiden name.

Ruby stopped moving for a moment and stared at Dorie with her mouth slightly open. She must have been about thirteen, but she looked like she was wearing makeup and her hair was cut into a bob that made her look older.

Chester wandered over to Ruby, butting his nose into her hand, greedy for affection. When she tried to push him away, he started to bark again, eager to play. Ruby yelled above the commotion, ignoring Chester's pleas. "Mom, can Sophie stay for lunch?"

Her friend hovered in the background until Sara responded. Dorie experienced an absurd twinge of jealousy as she watched the two girls grin when she said yes and link arms as they ran up the stairs, followed closely by Chester.

Sara turned to Dorie. "Will you be joining us?"

Dorie could see that Sara was trying to be kind, but a hard knot twisted Dorie's insides. "I need to get going." Dorie was suddenly superfluous, as if she'd interrupted a private gathering, rather than the other way around.

"I'll walk you out," said Hugh, leading her through the front door. Dorie rummaged in her purse for the car keys, not sure how to say goodbye. When he leaned in to give her a hug, his scent was so familiar that the intimacy was almost obscene. She pulled away too quickly, and he looked down at her as if for the last time.

return to bolivar peninsula

Moonshine marked her way as Clementine rode the boat back to the other side. There, she found a dark dune and slept under the condemnation of the stars. Only after the stars faded into submission did she continue, her skin and hair stiff with sand and salt, parched like the desert. She'd become a strange sea creature that had crawled from the ocean, lying desiccated on the shore. Her tracks marked the sand for him to follow, so he could find her if she lost her way. She stepped over the ocean's discarded innards: tangled coils of rope like entrails, viscera from the sea, bleached vertebrae like ancient relics.

When night fell again, she would follow the moon that sat low on the water, the black tarp punctured by stars, invisible seam between sea and sky. The moon would show her the way if she asked. She just had to look where it glinted on the water.

Almost there.

I will find you. I just have to watch the moonglow and listen very carefully.

ten things i love

and ten things i hate

*d*orie nervously checked the piece of paper with Shelley's address written on it, which Rennie had given her, but she couldn't have possibly missed the house—bubblegum pink covered nearly every surface. She parked in the driveway and took a deep breath before knocking on the door, not wanting to reveal her doubts about tutoring Izzie. But after visiting Hugh, Dorie had promised herself that she would try harder to become part of her new community. And she would start by helping out Rennie and Shelley.

A teenage girl like a Dickensian street urchin stood in the open doorway. She looked both childlike and world-weary in her skintight black jeans and skimpy tank top, her wrists wrapped in what looked like leather bandages, her nails scuffed and black.

"Hi, are you Izzie? I'm Dorie." Izzie let her in with a mumbled greeting and led her into the kitchen. The house looked as disheveled as Shelly had when Dorie met her at Coconuts. "Is your mom not home?"

"She's at work."

They sat at a small round table crowded with a dirty plate and glass and a stack of bills.

"So, what are you working on at the moment?" Dorie asked. "In school."

"Nothing, really."

"Well, what book has your teacher assigned this semester?"

"Um, *To Kill a Mockingbird.*"

One of Dorie's favorites. She experienced a flutter of excitement. But Izzie didn't have the book in front of her or anything to write on, for that matter.

"And how do you like it?"

"It's okay. I don't really get it, I guess."

"What do you mean? Have you read it?"

"Yeah, some. Sort of."

"Can you tell me what it's about?" Izzie looked around the kitchen, distracted or else avoiding eye contact. Dorie was suddenly aware of her vulnerability, her need to be seen. "Okay. I'll tell you what. Let's talk about something else before we get into the school stuff. What do you like to do?"

Izzie paused and bit at her cuticles. "Nothing, really."

"If you could do anything you wanted tomorrow, what would it be?"

"To be left alone."

"You enjoy being by yourself?"

"I'm *never* by myself. Mom always needs me to help with my brothers and stuff. I never get to do what I want."

"That must be very frustrating. It's a lot of responsibility for you."

"What are you, my therapist?"

Dorie bristled slightly at her tone, but she was used to sarcastic teens from her years of teaching. She'd often felt like a therapist toward her students, something she and Hugh had in common.

"You must be of great help to your mom, though. It's hard for her."

Izzie flared up. "I *know* it's hard for her!"

"Perhaps this time we spend together could be a way for you to have something for yourself."

Izzie gave her that contemptuous look that all teens perfected. "Are you kidding me! This isn't for me. This is just Mom and Uncle Rennie deciding I need to do better in school and making me do even *more* work."

Dorie realized then that she was in for a tough sell. She'd have to carefully lure Izzie in, like catching a fish fighting to break lose. "Listen. We'll start slow and see how it goes. If it doesn't work out, we'll stop after four sessions. Will you commit to four sessions with me?"

"Whatever," she mumbled.

"All right. Now, let's both make a list—'ten things I love and ten things I hate.' I'll give you fifteen minutes to compose your list, longer if you need it. Then perhaps we can share."

Izzie rolled her eyes.

Dorie tore a few sheets from her notepad and slid them toward Izzie, who picked up a pen from the clutter on the table. Her left hand hovered over the page, her right hand at her mouth, where she chewed on her nails. Dorie made two columns and then listed three things in the Love column: *Harriet, books, the ocean.* Then she moved to the Hate column, easily listing three more things: *cancer, being sad, lost children.*

Lost children—Finn—Clementine.

She added another two to the Hate column: *being alone, silence.* Then she realized that they also belonged in the Love column.

Izzie still wasn't writing.

"Can you not think of anything?"

Izzie paused, avoiding eye contact. "Can I not show you? What I write?"

"That's fine. I promise you can keep it to yourself for as long as you need. Just write them down, and it'll be a good start."

Izzie began scratching out words on the paper, her left hand moving with unfettered purpose, her right arm covering her words. Dorie recognized a humming intensity barely contained and recalled her own teenage years, when life consisted of moments of either deadening boredom or acute sensitivity, with not much in between. Would Harriet have been the same way? She'd always been such a quiet, sensitive girl, it was hard to imagine her rebelling like this. Dorie felt her stomach tighten and attempted to focus on Izzie.

After ten minutes, Izzie stopped writing, dropping her pen to the table. "Okay, I'm done."

"Now, I want you to examine your list and pick one item—just one—and expand on it. For instance, I wrote *the ocean* in my Love column."

Izzie rolled her eyes again.

"I'm going to start listing everything I love about the ocean: the sound of the waves, how the color changes all the time as if it had moods, the power of it . . . and the unpredictability of that power . . ."

An image of Finn being dragged under by the waves, farther and farther from the shore, flashed through her mind. Then Clementine's frozen face as she looked up to see him gone, knowing it was already too late but frantically battling the current as she searched for him anyway. Dorie suddenly felt the pull of the waves herself, the desperation . . .

The sound of Izzie shifting in her chair pulled Dorie back. As her vision cleared, she realized that Izzie was leaning slightly forward, her lips parted, watching her. Dorie looked down and tucked her hair behind her ears.

"Sorry, I got distracted."

"I know the feeling."

Dorie cleared her throat. "But that's really the point, isn't it? Ideas trigger other ideas, sometimes unexpected ones. If that happens, go with it. Try to delve further. Why don't you try working on that for a bit?"

Dorie looked back at her list and realized that the ocean also belonged in both columns. *Do we hate all the things that we love, to some degree?* She loved moments alone, when it was by choice. But she also knew that being truly alone could be a form of death, when the soul was no longer part of the living world.

They both wrote, Dorie forgetting herself in a scuffing cacophony of ideas, until she realized they'd gone well over their one-hour tutoring session.

"Okay, Izzie. Time's up."

Izzie stopped writing and dragged her eyes away from the paper toward Dorie. She looked a bit dazed. Dorie recognized that feeling, like being pulled from a dream.

"Keep working on the prewriting, and see what you can do with it."

"Do with it?"

"Try writing a narrative based on your notes. Or a poem, even."

"I don't know how to write a poem."

"Well, that's something we can work on, if you like." Dorie began packing up her things to leave. Izzie rolled her eyes one more time. "I'll see you the same time next week," she said as Izzie shut the door behind her.

onward

Clementine stayed close to where the waves touched the sand, wetting her foot so it stayed clean, unsullied by the seaweed stink and rotting carcasses that littered the shore. It was her affinity with them that permitted her to disappear, though. She listened to the muffled waves—listened for him as she trudged onward. She longed only for his world, under the green translucency, where they could finally reunite and become one again.

It will be very, very soon, mi vida.

clementine doesn't live

here anymore

*t*he weather had turned, and echoes of thunder threatened rain. Dark clouds shadowed the leaden sea, and immense pelicans headed west in slow motion as they attempted to outrun the storm.

Dorie and Rosie were bundled under a blanket on the couch, attempting to stay warm without any central heating. She'd put off the decision about the heating situation, not wanting to believe the HVAC repairman when he'd said she needed to replace the entire system. Even though she'd been told during the inspection when she bought the house that it was old and on its last legs, she'd hoped it would last a few more years.

The estimate for the new system made her pulse quicken, as she knew she'd have to cut corners and make extra money. She really didn't want to call John and ask for an editing job. He'd know she was desperate and would try to hand off something deadly boring that no one else wanted.

Hopefully I can last the rest of the winter without fixing it, then maybe save up over the year.

Dorie shivered, pulling Rosie closer to her for warmth. Then she turned her attention back to Clementine's journal, from which she read aloud to Rosie.

March 18, 2004

Today, Finn asked me where his daddy was. I told him he was away on an adventure at sea. What sort of adventure? He's on a quest to reverse a dark spell that was cast on him that keeps him from those he loves. Us? Yes. Will he come back? I don't know. That depends on whether he succeeds in his quest. What's a quest? It's a sort of test. I don't like tests. No, but he must be brave and strong if he wants to come home.

Rosie purred. "Shall I continue reading, or are you sleeping?" Dorie stroked Rosie's head. Rosie looked up at her and then over at the journal, as if wanting to hear more.

Love and hate make me seethe and cry. I don't want Finn to witness that. I don't want him to know what a bastard his father is and what a weak mess I am. Slivers of memory emerge, and I try to tell Finn just the good things about Lou: his beautiful face, his playful spirit, how he made me laugh until it hurt. How he sang me to sleep when I couldn't stop my mind from spinning. How I still cry whenever I hear a Johnny Cash song.

A loud crack of thunder and blaze of lightning preceded the clatter of rain. Rosie darted out from under the blanket and headed for the bedroom, probably to hide under the bed. Dorie went to the window and watched pools of rain collect rapidly on the uneven boards of the deck, rinsing them clean of their guano splats. The house swayed on its tall stilts as the wind picked up, a slow dance to the rhythm of the rain.

Suddenly, she realized what she had thought was another rumble of thunder was actually footsteps, rapidly climbing the stairs. Dorie moved quickly away from the window, wondering why anyone sane would be out in such weather.

A loud knock on the front door made her jump, her heart pounding. Then she heard shuffling on the deck and a key being forced into the lock. The door handle rattled along with her nerves as she tried to recall whether she'd locked it.

The door swung open violently, and a tall, stocky man stood framed in the doorway, a huge duffel bag slung across his broad shoulders. Rain flattened his hair close to his head and dripped from his eyelashes. He clutched a forlorn bunch of daisies wrapped in cellophane.

"Who are you?" His body shook with adrenaline that suddenly had no place to go. He threw his bag onto the floor and moved toward her, his bulk overwhelming the small space. "Where is she?"

"You need to leave. Or I'm calling the cops," Dorie said, a feeble attempt to sound in control.

"This is my house. What are you doing here, and where the hell is she?" He started for the bedroom, and Dorie considered running out into the rain to save herself from this madman. "Where's Clem?"

Dorie stiffened at the sound of her name. *Lou?* He was exactly as she had pictured him when reading Clementine's journal. His chalk face, hooded eyes hiding under a thatch of dark hair, brought to mind a Brontë hero—Heathcliff or Mr. Rochester.

"Clementine doesn't live here anymore," she said, her tone a warning. Part of her willed him to leave, while another wondered what Lou could tell her about Clementine.

"Where'd she go?"

Dorie clenched her jaw, exhausted by this unending question that no one seemed able to answer. "I don't know." She tried to lead him to the front door, her heart hammering.

"Wait. Just tell me how I can contact her." Lou held out the flowers; when she didn't reach for them, they hovered aimlessly. "She didn't write me back. I made my way here as soon as I got out." The stream of words tumbled from his mouth.

Dorie remembered the opened letter from Lou that she'd found: *Give him a kiss for me, and know I'll be home soon and that I think about you both every day.* Her shoulders sagged in resignation, and she gestured to a nearby chair. "Here, sit. I'll make you some hot tea."

She hoped it was safe to leave Lou alone in the living room. Eyeing her cell phone, she hesitated and then called the only person she could think of to help her.

"Oh my god," said Lynn in a panic after Dorie quickly explained. "Ken's out of town! I'm calling Rennie." She hung up before Dorie could respond.

When she returned to the living room, Lou was standing next to the window, surveying the room. She handed him a mug. "Here, drink this."

"I haven't heard from her in months." He held the mug of tea by the handle as if he didn't know what to do with it. "And then I was told about—"

An animal sound escaped his throat. His hand shook and tea spilled, the scald causing him to drop the mug. He rubbed his hand against his leg. Dorie returned to the kitchen for a towel, relieved to be away from the discomfort of watching Lou. When he continued, his voice scratched like an old record.

"I tried all I could to reach her. I figured if I could just see her . . ."

Dorie picked up the mug and began wiping the floor. "I told you, I don't know where she is."

"When did you last see her?" The air was charged, vibrating with his need.

"I haven't seen her. I don't even know her. Not really . . ." Standing up, the towel wet and limp in her hand, she twisted its corner between her fingers. "No one knows where she is."

"I need a drink."

"I can make more tea."

"I said I need a goddamn drink!"

Dorie backed away from him, squeezing the towel tightly in her fists to stop her hands from shaking. "I'll see what I can find."

In the kitchen, she rummaged through cupboards, taking longer than necessary so she could collect herself. She thought she might have some brandy left over from Christmas, when she had sat alone among a clutter of boxes and empty spaces.

When Dorie returned with the half-empty brandy bottle and a glass, Lou wasn't there, and she was momentarily relieved. Then she saw him through the window, huddled against the house under the awning, sucking on a cigarette as if his life depended on it. She considered putting the chain on the door, but as she made her way toward it, Lou saw her and threw down his cigarette, reentering the house.

She was horrified to see Clementine's journal tucked under his arm. Lou wiped raindrops from the cover and held it for several seconds before opening it. He stared at it for a long time and then reached for the brandy bottle, filling the glass, which he then gulped down in one quick move, already thirsty for another.

"I don't understand. Why do you have this?"

"She left it here."

Lou sat down in an armchair next to her and poured himself another glass, his size suffocating, as tobacco mixed with the smell of confinement. His face was a montage of emotions as he turned the pages. His brow creased, he shook his head, and then he rubbed his hand roughly over his face, as if trying to erase what he'd just seen. Dorie longed to snatch the book, reclaim it.

A loud knock at the front door cracked the tension, and Rennie came in, seeming to assess the crazed man who took up far too much space.

"Rennie. This is Lou." Her voice rasped. "He's looking for Clementine." She calculated the tenuous balance in the room.

"I'm sorry." Rennie stepped between Dorie and Lou. "But you won't find any answers here."

Lou stood up, towering over both Dorie and Rennie, and looked around. "This is my home. Where the hell is all our stuff?" He began moving about the room, picking up objects, opening the hall closet.

"It's time to leave," said Rennie, reaching for Lou's arm.

He pulled away violently. "Take your goddamn hands off me!" His eyes were glazed. "I'm staying here. I'm going to wait for her right here."

Dorie looked from Lou to Rennie, gauging the urgency of their next move.

"No, Lou. Let's go."

Lou's face darkened. "I said I'm not *leaving*." He pounded the wall with his fist, and a print Dorie had hung earlier that day fell to the ground with a shatter of glass.

Rennie held both hands up in the air as if in surrender. Then he looked at Dorie. "It might be time to call the cops."

Lou took a deep breath and blew it out slowly until he stilled. His voice was hollow. "What if she comes back and I'm not here?"

"We'll let you know if she shows up," Rennie said calmly. "We're going now. Come on." He picked up Lou's bag and held it out to him. "Dorie, are you going to be okay?"

She nodded.

"Where am I supposed to go?" Lou asked.

"You can stay at my place for the night, and then tomorrow, we'll figure out what to do."

Lou pulled his bag from Rennie's grasp and walked out the door, into storm clouds low on the horizon. Rennie followed behind.

Dorie quickly locked the door and put on the safety chain. She heaved a sigh that stuck midway up her chest as her eyes rested on the wilted flowers that were wedged between the cushions of the couch, Clementine's journal next to them. Dorie picked up the journal and wiped its surface. She flipped through the pages, knowing the pain Lou must have felt reading Clementine's words.

That's when she realized the sketch of Finn was gone.

infinite particles

Clementine squeezed the rock tighter in her fist, until the edges marked her palm, a deep crevice, another lifeline. *Dark with wet, heavy and solid like my heart.* She threw it hard into the sand.

No more lifelines.

A sand crab scuttled sideways, a ghost barely visible in the waning light.

Where will you go? Into your dark hole, waiting still and silent for a bite, lingering patiently until darkness falls? Do you feel the rhythm of the tide inside your sabulous chamber? Do you move with the ebbing and waning, for eternity? Is he there with you? One of the infinite particles, one with the tides, one with the sea itself?

I am here, mi corazón.

the visible and invisible touch

*D*orie sat on the deck, sipping from the second glass of wine she'd been nursing for the past hour, a remedy for her insomnia that she relied on more than she'd like to admit. A pathway of light cast from the full moon separated the dark water below. She pulled her coat tightly around herself against the chill of the night air. It was the time of night when the visible and the invisible touched. When the rest of the world slept and she counted the hours one by one, waiting for the oblivion of sleep.

Suddenly, her eyes registered movement, a lone figure in the darkness near the shore. Her pulse quickened, her senses on high alert, as though a switch had been turned on.

She sprang from the chair, her leaden legs dragging her through the night. As she clambered over the dunes, they almost gave way beneath her, and she struggled not to slip. She reached the water and gasped as the icy waves reached higher, the farther she went. Wading in slow motion, Dorie followed the moonshine that lit her way, the water pushing hard against her as she drew closer to the figure.

Then, without a sound, it disappeared.

Frantically propelling herself forward, battling the waves, Dorie searched blindly under the water. Salt water forced its way into her mouth until she choked and spluttered. Seaweed wound about her legs, as if it wanted to engulf her.

Finally, she reached out and felt cold flesh. Talons tore at her arm and hair as she pulled. The form was almost weightless—a spirit, an otherworldly creature, rather than a living, breathing person. Dorie's toes gripped the silty surface beneath the waves, and she dragged with all her strength, until they'd both reached the shore and collapsed upon the hard, wet sand.

Dorie rolled onto her back, facing the stars. After taking a few deep breaths to calm herself, she turned her head. Yes, human. But barely.

Her pale body shone silver in the dark, wet hair a mass of black tresses, like the seaweed that had impeded their progress through the black waves to the shore. But Dorie somehow knew it was Clementine, had known before she even reached the waves, whose grasp she'd struggled to pull her from.

"Clementine?" Dorie reached for her. "I want to help you."

Clementine sat up. "I have to find him. He's calling . . ."

Dorie gripped Clementine's arms and spoke over her in breathless bursts. "I live just up there." She pointed to the yellow house. "Come with me," she implored, taking Clementine's hands in hers.

Clementine looked up at the house. "Is he there?"

It was then that the cold registered and Dorie began to shiver violently, her wet clothes clinging to her body. She stood and lifted Clementine to her feet. Clementine let Dorie lead her across the dunes, along the starlit path, up the stairs, and into the light.

Clementine pulled the blanket closer, over her ears, shivering. *So cold even now, in this cursed light.* Through the window, she could see the too-far-away waves in the moonlight, the feral sea that had claimed her boy.

"Clementine, here, drink this." Her Keeper placed something steaming on the table, its wood grains swirling like currents. Clementine rubbed her finger along a depression, a wound, diagonal and deep—*Finn pressing his fork into the wood, pressing, pressing. Me yelling, yanking it out of his hand.* That dark crevice was a scar that she now probed with her finger. Her Keeper's metallic voice pressed through the too-still air, drowning out the other voices, the ones she needed to hear so she could find him. Her voice so insistent, scratching at Clementine's ears to be let in.

Her Keeper made her drink, tiny sips. Then she stood. "You need to rest. Come." She reached for Clementine, tugged gently at her arm. But Clementine remembered the way, down the darkened passage to the bedroom, where she closed the door to shut her Keeper out.

Clementine removed the wetness, like peeling off her skin, layer by layer. But it didn't hurt, only revealed her deformities, the grotesque monster she was. Crawling into bed, long forgotten but suddenly so familiar, she burrowed into the darkest corners to dream again of her lost boy.

selkie

*F*ate had finally brought them together.

Dorie looked at Clementine's wasted form, which barely made an impression under the covers, her matted hair resembling an animal. *Will she transform in the night, a selkie I should have left in the sea where she belongs?*

Dorie left the bedroom door slightly ajar and went to the kitchen, looking for the bottle of brandy she'd offered Lou. As she took a sip, her insides spread with a heat that burned and comforted simultaneously. All that time spent reading Clementine's innermost thoughts, knowing her almost better than Dorie knew herself, had led to this moment.

But what do I do with her now?

Dorie reached for the phone and dialed Rennie's number. He answered in a voice groggy with sleep. "Rennie, I'm sorry to call so late," she said, glancing at the clock.

"What's wrong?" he asked, sounding more alert.

"Clementine's here." Rennie took a long, slow breath, as if sorting through his sleep-addled mind for her name. "Lou's girlfriend, wife . . ." She struggled with the frustration of having to explain who Clementine was when she didn't really know herself. Dorie thought of Clementine curled up in her bed, hiding from the world and from herself.

"She's in your house?"

"Yes. She was down by the water . . . I didn't know what else to do, so she's here."

"Listen, why don't I come over." She heard shuffling sounds. "We can talk properly."

"Is Lou still staying with you?"

"No. He's staying with a friend of mine."

"On the peninsula?" Dorie asked, hoping he'd left and moved on.

"Yeah. Pete hired him on for a while to help out with his shrimp business."

She heard keys rattle in the background. Well, at least Lou wasn't around to watch Rennie's comings and goings, to ask unwanted questions.

"I'll be there in five minutes," Rennie said, right before he hung up.

Dorie wanted him to come but didn't like that she did. She took another sip of brandy and collapsed onto the sofa. Tomorrow, she'd figure out where to take Clementine, to get her the help she needed.

She must have dozed off because she was startled awake by a knock on the door. She prayed it was Rennie, not Lou somehow knowing already that Clementine was there.

"Dorie? You okay?"

Recognizing Rennie's voice, Dorie rushed to the door and let him in. Then she panicked, worried that Clementine had left while she dozed. Rennie followed her to the bedroom, where Clementine's childlike body was curled under the blanket in a fetal position, Rosie snuggled against her. Dorie smoothed the blanket, a gesture so familiar to her, from so long ago. Rennie watched her as if he knew.

They went into the kitchen, where she filled the coffee-pot with water and several scoops of ground coffee, knowing she wouldn't be able to sleep anyway.

"What are you going to do?" Rennie's face was creased with concern. Dorie opened the cabinet and sorted through her crowded mug collection, clattering them against each other, then worried that she'd wake Clementine. She felt Rennie's eyes on her as he spoke again. "I'm just worried you might be taking on more than you can handle."

Dorie paused, unsure if she was angry or grateful. "Well, I don't know that I *am* taking her on." Rennie walked over to the window, where the outside floodlights accentuated the lines of his face. "And you can't tell Lou she's here, okay? Not yet." She thought of all the sealed letters that Clementine hadn't opened. "I just want her to have a little time to get stronger first."

Rennie turned from the window to face her. "Not to say he won't find out, though. You know how it is around here." She could imagine. It was only a matter of time. "Maybe you should call social services."

"Maybe. But they'd just keep her for a while, and then she'd be back out on the streets again."

"What about her family? Can't they take her?"

"I don't know anything about her family."

Rennie's shoulders rose as he took a breath and sighed.

"I think I may need to keep her for a while."

He frowned. "Keep her? You make her sound like a stray dog you picked up."

Her jaw tightened, Rosie flashing through her mind. "I mean help her. Let her stay here with me for a few days, until

I can figure something out." A silence fell between them, only the distant waves making it bearable. "I'm not sure she's interacted with anyone who knows her, or cares, in a very long time."

"And you know her and care?" Rennie asked.

Dorie looked away from him. It was the first time he'd made her feel diminished, but she refused to shrink before him.

His voice turned low and controlled. "Just be careful. You don't know what she might do."

"For God's sake, Rennie. She's broken. She's not a threat to anyone but herself."

The coffee maker beeped, and Dorie forced herself to ask if he wanted a cup, willing him to leave.

"I don't think I will, thanks." He paused, his eyes on the coffee maker. "Perhaps I'll head out."

She walked him to the front door. "It'll be fine. Don't worry." Rennie nodded and walked away, Dorie locking the door behind him.

Suddenly, a sound like an injured animal's came from the bedroom. Dorie rushed to Clementine, who was sitting up in bed, the remnants of a nightmare visible—her fragility so raw, it hurt to look at her.

ablutions

•

Clementine dreamed she was painting again, brush-strokes layered green and blue, fluid like water. Streaks of silver—those hundred drops of mercury—his pale body floating among the silver fish as if he were one of them. Translucent green turned dark near the bottom of the canvas. She tried to keep the black down, bury it until only the light radiated up toward the surface, carrying him with it. But her fingers cramped, and the brush moved on its own, the dark rising from the depths, tendrils threatening to retrieve him. Until he disappeared, down, down into the black.

A sound escaped her lungs as she woke from that night-mare into another. Everything was bathed in golden light, shimmering with life. It entered from a window curtained in yellow.

I am still here.

In her room hung the sailboat painting she'd done for Finn so long ago. And Tabitha, her cat, who stood on the bed looking dazed at having been woken so abruptly. She peered at Clementine and then nudged her head against her chin.

103

Perhaps I'm still dreaming and can summon Finn, bring him back into the light with me. The ghost of her animal wail rinsed the gold from the room as she heard footsteps. *Someone is here— Lou? Has he come back for me?*

But when the bedroom door opened, her Keeper peered around it. Clementine let out the breath she'd been holding.

She looks frightened. Of me?

She should be.

I am.

Clementine rose from the bed, shivering in her nakedness. The air was filled with a salty funk—primeval sweat and rot.

Her Keeper handed her a robe that was breath against her skin, speaking in the hushed tones of a cleric. "How about a hot bath?" She led her by the elbow, barely touching. She turned on the water and tested the temperature with an outstretched hand. "Here's a towel, soap, shampoo. Okay?"

As if I don't understand.

Clementine reluctantly removed the robe, ashamed again of her stinking nakedness. Her Keeper watched her still, so she stepped into the tub, showing that she knew how to be human. Finally, her Keeper left her alone, leaving the door partway open.

The shock of hot water was thorns on her skin. She immersed herself, covering her body, her face, opening her mouth as if she could drown. The white ceiling undulated above the transparent water as if she were buried in glass. But she couldn't hold her breath any longer and emerged into the chill of white tiled walls and floor. She turned on the hot again, until she felt she might be swallowed by hellfire.

As if from very far away, a tentative knock came at the door, and then her Keeper's voice. "Are you okay in there?"

Clementine rose and splashed so her Keeper knew she was still there, holding onto the sides of the tub to keep from sinking under. She forced herself back into that space, that strange halfway world that her Keeper insisted she reenter. She lathered her hair, her scalp, scrubbed her skin raw until it reddened and burned.

When her Keeper returned, the water was tepid, so that Clementine was no longer aware of it against her skin—her blood and the water both indiscernible. *Unlike the sea, which never lets me forget we are divided, never lets me lose myself in its embrace.* She shivered as her Keeper handed her a towel. Wrapping it about her shining wet body, she watched the water drain—a swirl of mud and grit.

Her Keeper looked at her like Clementine was hurting her. "Are you hungry? I made you a sandwich."

Clementine turned her back and walked to the bedroom, calling her cat's name and closing the door.

secrets

Clementine was sleeping, so Dorie cleaned the house, her body needing work to help still her mind.

Why did she call Rosie Tabitha, as if she knew her?

On her hands and knees, she scrubbed at the black mark Clementine had left on the tub, rinsed away the filth she'd endured. Her hands stung from the bleach, her fingers raw. Dorie recalled the tattoo she'd glimpsed on Clementine's back when she removed the robe. It was a yin-yang symbol, like the one Dorie had found in the sand the morning after the magical green lights in the waves. Had Clementine been there that night? How often had she visited the shore by the little yellow house, while Dorie sat inside, devouring her words?

The house seemed even quieter with Clementine in it. Dorie tiptoed about, moved things carefully, swept instead of vacuumed, so as not to disturb her. Dorie didn't know how to be with Clementine when she was awake, so she let her sleep.

As she dusted the bookcase, Dorie saw Clementine's

journal sitting atop a pile of books. Her impulse was to hide it. But when she picked it up, it was as if Clementine were speaking her secrets aloud, so softly, Dorie couldn't make out the words and had to look inside to be sure.

June 6, 2004

It's my birthday today. Lou sent a card. I wanted to throw it away but couldn't quite bring myself to. But I will.

The unopened letters that had been with Clementine's journal were now in Dorie's desk, away from sight. Away so she wouldn't be tempted to open them, as she had been countless times. Perhaps she should put the journal and letters somewhere Clementine could happen upon them, never knowing Dorie had found them, read them.

Not yet, though.

No card from Dad, of course. I wonder if he ever thinks of me. Not that we celebrated any of my twenty-four birthdays. It's a day he'd rather erase completely—the day he lost her. I suppose he just erased me instead.

Had she lost her mother as well? How much could a person bear? More than anyone would think possible. A feat that still astounded her—the fact that she hadn't died when her daughter did.

Finn and I baked a cake, and he gave me a shell he'd found on the beach. Said it was the very best one. I put it on a piece of string and told him I'd wear it close to my heart, where he would always be.

Dorie tried to remember if Clementine had been wearing the shell when she found her. She hoped so. She flipped through the pages, until her eyes landed on the word *father*.

December 20, 2003

Lou keeps writing and calling. I'm surprised by his perseverance. He seemed so reluctant to be a father. I suppose he didn't have the best role model, though.

Why is my life filled with reluctant fathers? Is fatherhood such a difficult duty to fulfill? Being a mother doesn't come easy to me, but my love for Finn supersedes all doubt.

When I was pregnant, Lou was so gentle with me, took such good care of me—while I was still all his. I'll never forget his face the first time he saw Finn. It wasn't love I saw in his eyes; it was panic. That's when he started slowly disappearing from our lives.

I'm actually sort of relieved he's in prison. I'm not sure I could send him away if he showed up here. I miss him. No, not him—my version of him. The best of him is still with me: Finn. His laugh, his hands, his sense of exploration. I can't decide what's worse: Finn having Lou as his father or not having a father at all.

Even though I never knew what it was to have a mother, I came close with Maria. Although she earned a paycheck to raise me, I think she truly cared for me. My father certainly wasn't enough to fill that ache. But I will be enough for Finn—mi vida. It's just him and me now; we don't need anyone else.

Last night, I watched him sleep, breathed in his boy scent, my heart brimming. He's enough. More than enough.

Slowly peeking over her right shoulder, Dorie almost expected to find Clementine standing there, her face a mix of outrage and disappointment. Dorie closed the book and stayed very still, listening for her.

Dorie went to bed early that night but couldn't sleep, as usual. Her whole body ached from cleaning the house. She missed Rosie snuggling against her and resented that she seemed to prefer a stranger.

Or is she a stranger?

That's when it hit her: Rosie was Clementine's cat, Tabitha. She'd abandoned her along with this house and whatever else she'd left behind. Perhaps it wasn't that Rosie preferred Clementine but that she knew she needed her more than Dorie did.

Staring into the Picasso shadows cast about the room, she waited for Clementine's cries. Just as she used to wait for Harriet's. It was when Harriet was a baby that Dorie first lost the ability to sleep long and hard; she would wake every three hours for her feeds. And when she got sick, Dorie would listen for her in the night because she hadn't wanted to miss it when Harriet needed her.

She had watched Harriet fade, day by day. Near the end, she'd asked Dorie, "Mom, are pets allowed into heaven? Will Daisy be there?"

Dorie had given her the only possible response: "Yes."

Harriet had closed her eyes. "Good." Her voice had been a thread of gossamer lost among the outside noises coming in the open hospital room window. Then she'd opened her eyes and looked into Dorie's fractured face. "I'm sorry, Mom."

As sleep crept slowly closer, Dorie returned to the bench in the garden at MD Anderson where she and Harriet had sat early on in her daughter's treatment. Dorie read the inscription on the bench, pitying the parents who had lost their child. Harriet was wrapped in a blanket, even in the oppressive heat of a Texas summer. They watched clouds pass overhead—a dragon, a sheep, an angel.

Then the bench transformed into the one that Hugh's practice had donated, bearing its own inscription. She hated that bench—bleached gray, scarred with graffiti, splitting in the Texas heat. Dorie felt it rot slowly beneath them, until it was replaced with another bench commemorating the life of another lost child. Over and over and over again.

blank slate

*C*lementine paused at the front door of the house and listened, but sleeping sounds were the only ones she could hear. *I don't belong in the glare and stifling warmth of this sterile place. With this stranger who always looks at me too hard.*

Turning the lock, she was surprised that it submitted and she could walk away. *Not a prison after all.*

Outside was a blank slate, the world erased. A pale sky held the sun, wrapped in a shroud, only halfway above the tear between sea and sky. When she reached the dunes, a V of gulls drifted into view, searching for a resting place, and then vaporized like ghosts. Fog enveloped her, and she was contained within it, separated from the world outside. She stepped onto the sand, and it sunk, accepting her imprint, her sole marking her tracks to the water.

The tide would soon erase her so she could be invisible once more.

A bloom of jellyfish spread out across the sand, their fluorescent blue incongruous against the gray world, like an old colorized photograph. They drifted with the tides, unable to direct their own fates. Left only to wash up on the shore to die, evaporating into nothingness.

They resembled their namesake—Medusa—long tentacles like her head of writhing snakes that transformed her victims to stone. The once-beautiful maiden punished for lying with Poseidon, turned into a monster.

Perhaps I too have seen her face and that is why I'm no longer a warm-blooded woman but a dull gray mass, solid and cold.

I am not of this world. Of my Keeper's world.

Panting, she inhaled the moist air, her hair sprinkled with minuscule droplets like scattered jewels. She listened for him—*Why is he not calling to me?* Stepping into the green-gray sludge, Clementine looked far off to where the water began to turn clear. *Is he there, where fish dart and new sunlight rips seams in the blue?*

There—she heard her name being called. She listened again. But it wasn't coming from the water. Clementine turned her head and heard it again, closer now, coming from the beach. A figure emerged from the fog.

Finn!

She ran from the water toward him, her breath in bursts, her heart thudding until it filled her chest, smothering her.

"Clementine! What are you doing out here? For god's sake!" Her Keeper reached out.

Not him, then. Never him.

Clementine pulled away, stumbling over sand that gave way beneath her as it did in nightmares.

"Come back with me. Just for a little while."

"Stay away from me!" Clementine wailed.

"Please, just until you feel a bit stronger."

Their voices clashed over the waves, a discordant symphony. Clementine didn't even turn to look at her as she tossed obscenities over her shoulder, into the sand for her

Keeper to pick up. Over and over, until she had no will left to fight.

No will to even stop living.

Then her Keeper was in front of her, blocking her way, forcing her to stillness.

"I understand."

Her Keeper's eyes bored into hers, through the blur of muddled thoughts floating in Clementine's vision. Never clearing. Until Clementine saw her pain.

"My daughter. I lost her too."

So she too had transformed—a creature hollowed out, scraped bare. Clementine stepped forward, looked closer at her Keeper through the mist.

Yes, I see that now. We are the same.

Clementine followed her Keeper. Tears wet her face, warm against the cold dewdrops. Stumbling blindly, she heard their breath mix with the sodden air, until the yellow house finally appeared, shining through the mist.

Clementine wrapped her hands around a mug of hot tea and brought it to her face, wanting desperately to be warm again. Tabitha jumped into Clementine's lap, and they all sat within the silence. Clementine looked around the room, so familiar yet so different.

"Who are you, and why are you in my house? With my cat?" Her voice grated like rusty hinges forced open.

"I'm Dorie. This is my house now." She locked her eyes on Tabitha as if that alone could reclaim her. "And I didn't know Rosie was—"

"Tabitha," Clementine corrected, stroking the purring cat's head. Clementine couldn't see any remnants of herself in this place except Tabitha. Her life had been erased, like the gray world outside. The only furniture that remained was the table by the kitchen window, where she used to sit with the two she had loved.

Her eyes landed on a photo of a young girl, the frame lost among rows of books crammed into the bookcase.

Dorie looked up and followed her gaze. "That's my daughter, Harriet."

Clementine felt for Finn's shell at her throat, rubbed its ridges, anticipating each dip and crevice.

"She was eight when she died." Dorie's voice was lost in the expanse of the room, as if it had taken the wrong path to reach Clementine's ears.

Clementine looked outside. The fog had lifted slightly, so the world appeared as if through a smudged lens. When she looked back at Dorie, she recognized her own face reflected back at her.

abstracted

*d*ays passed without time. Dorie slept late into the mornings, the light disorienting her when she opened her eyes. She still hadn't the heart to kick Clementine out of her bedroom and was making do with the guest room for now, so she felt displaced. They both ate tiny morsels, like rations, not speaking, so words lost their meaning and the world abstracted. They both read incessantly, consuming words as sustenance. Dorie immersed herself in the pages, a tonic for the despondency she felt over Clementine's separation from the real world.

The shrill sound of the phone ringing shattered the silence. Dorie rushed to answer it so it wouldn't wake Clementine. Hearing Rennie's voice loosened the rigidity in her shoulders, cut a cord that had been binding her.

"Is Clementine still there?"

"Yes." Her voice was fragmented, not her own.

"Shel said you haven't been showing up for Izzie's tutoring lessons."

"Oh God, I'm so sorry." She'd been wandering in a place

between this reality and another, so the real world had started to blur.

"It's okay. We were just worried." He paused as if assessing. "Do you need anything?"

She asked if he'd mind getting them some supplies—because they needed food and because she needed to speak aloud to someone.

Because she wanted to see him.

Clementine was still asleep when Rennie arrived with bags of groceries, which they unpacked silently. Then they shared whispers out on the deck so as not to disturb Clementine.

"How is she?"

"She still sleeps most of the time. But I got her to start eating a little more."

"And how are you? Really."

"I'm fine. Really," she lied.

"We all want to help here. You can't do this on your own."

Can't I? Perhaps not. She felt uneasy, didn't want Rennie to know how indebted she felt to him. But taking care of damaged girls was the only thing she seemed capable of.

"You need to take care of yourself," he said, as if reading her mind. Rennie watched her silence, listened acutely for its meaning. "At least take a walk. It'll make you feel better." Again, reading her thoughts. She longed to sink her feet into the cool underlayer of sand, to feel the salt-sticky film on her skin after dipping into the water. "I'll stay here until you get back." Dorie weighed her need for the release of a long, strenuous walk on the beach against the risk of Clementine waking to find Rennie there. "Go. Don't worry." She smiled faintly and thanked him as she reached for her coat and hat.

Walking across the dunes to the beach, she felt as if she'd awoken from a dream, released into a version of the world scrubbed clean, bright, and pure. The green hat that Harriet had knitted for her hugged her head, spreading warmth through her slightly graying hair, each stitch touched by her daughter's fingers.

She'd learned how to knit in the hospital during one of her longer stays. She'd been frustrated at first when her fingers fumbled with the needles and she'd drop stitches and lose count. Then she became so proficient that she could make a hat in less than an hour. She'd knitted hat after hat, baskets brimming. After completing their bloodwork, patients would get to pick out their favorite as a reward. A reward for being brave, for fighting the disease. For still being alive.

Unbuttoning her coat, Dorie invited in the chill of the late-winter air. Endless days between November and February offered patches of sunlight like gifts, warmth creeping through layers of wool to reach the skin beneath. Dorie ran to where the waves stroked the sand, remembering just in time to remove her shoes before she entered the water. Her feet tingled and fizzed. She stuffed her hat into a pocket lined with sand and a bleached bone like ivory that she'd forgotten was there. Splashing her face and hair reawakened senses that had numbed, been forced dull. She longed to immerse her entire body in the sea, rinse herself of the muck that was a barrier between her and this new place.

As Dorie continued walking, the pale February sun dried the last remnants of seawater, and her skin tightened, her hair crusted and curled. She increased her pace until her breath deepened and her limbs loosened. Spring was around the corner, and she held her face up to the sun in anticipation. A murmuration of starlings swept overhead, swirling in unison, a mourning veil of black crepe carried away by the wind.

Drawing closer to the bridge at Rollover Pass, she slowed

down. That strip of beach narrowed considerably and was more difficult to navigate. Up ahead, fishermen lined the man-made concrete walls to catch blacktip sharks, brown shrimp, and blue crabs carried by incoming tides from the bay, as well as freshwater speckled trout and hardhead catfish that rode the brackish outgoing tides. Dorie remembered reading that Rollover Pass was named for the way smugglers would roll barrels of rum and whiskey over the narrow stretch of land during Prohibition, avoiding Galveston customs officers.

A lone figure up ahead bent over a bulk of driftwood, like one of the ghost smugglers. He was wrapping a thick chain around a large tree trunk, his tall, wiry frame slicing the air. He dragged the end of the chain toward a black pickup truck parked between two dunes. Dorie stopped and watched him, pulled in by his movements and the need to fill the air with shared words.

"It's for my next project," he called when he noticed her, adjusting the blue bandanna wrapped around his head. His braided beard was streaked gold and silver, like the sea after a storm.

"What's your project?" she asked, intrigued by this man whose eyes spoke of ocean travels and untouched worlds.

"You should stop by my place on 87 and find out what this thing decides to become."

"Your place?"

He held out a calloused hand. "People call me the Tiki Man, but my name's Kevin."

Everyone on the peninsula knew the Tiki Man. He was an artist, a woodworker, whose outdoor studio was just west of The Big Store. His carved tikis were assembled along a grassy stretch nearby, guests at a party to which people really wanted to be invited.

He locked the chain securely onto the back end of the truck, pulling on it hard to make sure it would hold.

"It's not up to you, then? What this tree will become?"

"Seems not," he shrugged. "These trees have been around a long time, been through a lot—storms, hurricanes, traveled oceans. Those experiences make each one unique. I just listen and try to understand them."

"A tree whisperer?"

He laughed. "I like that."

He nodded and got into his truck. When he drove away, the tree creaked as the chain pulled taut, dislodging it from its resting place against the dune. A gash left half the dune freshly exposed, moist sand darker than the surface layer, which collapsed in slow motion until it was a ruined heap. Dorie turned to retrace her steps back to the house, hoping the figure that emerged under Kevin's hands justified the sand dune's sacrifice.

When Dorie got home, the house was quiet. Rennie looked up from a book he was reading.

"How was your walk?"

"It was good." She smiled as though she'd forgotten how until now. "Did Clementine wake up?"

"I'm not sure. I thought I heard something, but it's all fine."

Relieved, Dorie asked what he was reading. "Found it on the bookshelf over there." He stood to replace the book. "I didn't want the TV waking Clementine—figured I should keep quiet."

Dorie moved closer to look at the cover: *Of Mice and Men.* "You can borrow it, if you like."

"Thanks. I'll give it a go." He gestured to the shelf in front of him, which held Harriet's photo. "She yours?"

Dorie dreaded the question more than any other and had learned to edit her answer based on the person asking. "Yes. Harriet."

"How old?"

"She was five in that photo." Dorie hadn't shared much of herself with Rennie and wondered if now was the time. He waited patiently for her to go on, so she did. "She died four years ago—cancer."

Rennie's expression shifted. "I'm sorry to hear that."

He reached toward her, and she panicked, not sure what his touch might do. Rennie stepped back a fraction, seeming to sense her resistance, but he kept his eyes on her. Kind eyes that made her feel both stronger and more vulnerable at the same time.

"Remember, you have friends here." Dorie smiled, understanding that she needed to let him be her friend. "You don't have to do all this on your own." She nodded. "In fact, you don't have to do it at all." He stopped talking and looked at her, assessing her reaction.

"Just a little longer. Until she's stronger."

"Do you need to take a break from tutoring Iz?"

"Maybe just a couple of weeks, if that's okay. I'm really sorry about missing the last few sessions."

"Take your time. Just let Shel know. And let me know if I can help any."

"Okay." Perhaps she really did mean it this time.

forest of suicides

acing to catch me, round and round, my Keeper reaches the Seventh Circle. I disappear, but rounding the next ring, she sees me—my bark skin, slender trunk, arms bending into branches that push her away. My limbs shiver in anguish, dead leaves rattling curses.

She cries out to me, imploring me to tear my roots from the earth. But these roots run deep. I am damned to this place, this forest of suicides. I fall, down, down to the river Lethe, where my mind fogs.

Why do I race? For whom do I search?

Cocytus's frozen depths capture me, doom me to the Ninth Circle of Hell, where I stand frozen to my neck in Lucifer's tears—for betraying the one I've lost, the one I must save. Burning ice holds me still and fast, my chest compressed, my blood slowing but never stopping, never stopping. For eternity, I have only my clouded sight, my shallow breath, my feeble screams to search for them.

To save both our children.

Clementine woke with a trapped scream. She wondered if Dorie shared the same dream of saving their children. Reaching for a robe, she opened the bedroom door. A man sat in Dorie's chair. She silently closed the door again and clicked the lock. Then she sensed a presence at her door. Waiting, still and silent.

"Clementine?" His voice was a whisper. "Are you okay? I'm a friend of Dorie's. She'll be back soon."

Why is he here? In our house?

She checked the lock before creeping back to bed, breathing fast and shallow. Waiting for him to leave.

memento mori

*d*orie remembered seeing an easel in the garage that she suspected belonged to Clementine, and it gave her an idea. Perhaps Clementine could find herself again by painting, immersing herself in a long-familiar activity.

When Dorie was locked inside herself, Hugh had read to her. The sound of his voice had entered her consciousness like a salve, although she struggled to remember which books he had read. The words themselves hadn't registered at first, but he had persevered and slowly she'd found herself listening.

Later, Dorie realized that Hugh had chosen the books he had because they were a place of comfort for her, ones she knew well and had returned to many times in her life, before and after Harriet. She distinctly remembered the turning point, when he read from one of her favorite books of poems by Seamus Heaney.

She decided to get some painting supplies from Galveston. It was worth the risk of leaving Clementine there alone. She'd been doing better over the past couple of weeks, and anyway, Dorie was desperate for some time away on her own. She scribbled a note: *Running errands. Back soon, D.* It was still early, and Clementine slept late most days, so Dorie hoped she'd be back before Clementine got up.

At the end of Highway 87 near Port Bolivar, only a few cars were ahead of her in line for the ferry. During the summer months, it was best to avoid the ferry trip between Bolivar and Galveston. Only tourists were foolish enough to wait in line for two hours. But during off-season, there were fewer lines, and it was a nice boat trip across the bay.

A guide waved Dorie into the correct lane, and her car clanked over the loading ramp, announcing her arrival. Birds watched from their perches nearby, grooming disheveled plumage, occasionally grumbling to one another—they'd seen it all a million times. Equally bored guides in orange-and-silver vests waved on more passengers.

A loudspeaker competed with the drone of the engine, welcoming them aboard and stating the ferry rules: "no smoking," "stay in your vehicle until the ferry departs." The latter of which most people ignored. Then the horn signaled the ferry's departure, and seagulls congregated overhead, singing their ocean stories in exchange for scraps of bread.

Dorie hurried from the confines of her car, unlike most riders, who stayed inside at this time of year, protected from the stinging wind and wayward water. She preferred to stand on the deck, along with a handful of others brave enough to risk a soaking from the ferry's wake.

Soon, a young girl cried out. "I see one!" She pointed to a black fin and grabbed her mother's arm. No matter how many times people saw the dolphins, it was always a thrill. Like movie stars, they flaunted sleek, smooth bodies, smiling widely at all the attention.

The girl's mother placed her hands on her daughter's

shoulders, ready to switch their positions if a wave threatened. Dorie gripped the stern of the ferry and stared down at the muddy-brown depths. Parents fooled themselves into believing they could protect their children. She wondered how many mothers, fathers, sons, and daughters these depths had claimed.

Looming up ahead, the SS *Selma*'s torn hull exposed rusted innards, making it appear vulnerable despite its massive bulk. A concrete vessel launched in 1919, it had suffered irreparable damage and found its final resting place there, near Pelican Island. A man next to Dorie told his companion that it was a half-sunken pirate ship, that there had been treasure on it and the person who discovered it became a rich man—a friend of his, actually.

The ferry shared the water with numerous other vessels: behemoth tankards and barges, dazzling white cruise ships with waving passengers, shrimp boats and speedboats zipping by like windup toys. At Seawolf Park, a few fishermen tried their luck, shadowed by the USS *Cavalla*, a WWII submarine that lay in state.

When Dorie and Hugh had first discovered Bolivar, they visited tourist sites and read as many books as they could find about the area. She remembered feeling as if she were in on a secret, knowing so much about a place that so few other people knew existed, and it had made her passionate and protective of it.

Now that she actually lived there, she realized she was still very much an outsider peering through a lens.

After disembarking, Dorie continued down 87 for a bit. Small suburban bungalows and apartment complexes were cloistered by ragged palm trees and colorful oleanders. Along the Seawall, enormous hotels towered over streets semi-deserted at this time of year. A few tandem cyclists and skaters glided between bars and restaurants that sat relatively empty compared to the summer months, when they bulged at the seams.

She stopped at Walmart, where crowds of people with blank stares wandered the aisles like automatons. Dorie was soon overwhelmed after being cooped up with just Clementine for so long and hurried to finish her shopping.

She bought some canvases, paints, charcoal, and brushes and then decided to pick out some essentials for Clementine. She'd been wearing Dorie's clothes, as she had none of her own except what she'd worn the day Dorie found her. They hung off her, so that she resembled a small child lost inside her mother's clothes. But she didn't seem to give it a second thought.

Not knowing her taste or size, Dorie stuck to basics, but there was a certain pleasure in it. She was reminded of shopping for Harriet, trying to select items that accentuated her frail prettiness. It was with some relief, though, that she checked out and stowed her purchases in the trunk of her car.

Dorie had one more quick stop to make, to buy a gift for her nephew's birthday, but she'd need to hurry in case Clementine woke up soon. Broadway was a central artery of well-tended esplanades lined with grand homes that boasted of years past when Galveston was a major port and bustling destination city.

Dorie found a free parking spot near the Strand, and soon she stood among nineteenth century architecture: an assortment of tall, sturdy brick buildings, some scuffed and boarded up with ghost impressions of painted signs on the walls, others meticulously restored with ornate stone moldings and large mullioned windows.

She stepped over metal tracks inlaid along the red brick streets that once carried clanging trolleys. These tracks lay dormant now but had once dictated the trolleys' path through the downtown Strand area to the Seawall. She could almost feel the surge of those shiny conduits, as if they still carried the pulse of travelers journeying from the bustling town to the lull of the sea.

Suddenly, she shuddered, imagining Clementine stepping over these same tracks, lost and alone.

Hendley Market was a bit off the tourist track and a fascinating place to poke around in. Odd assortments of porcelain doll parts and ancient medical instruments brought to mind gruesome scenes of morphine-hazed surgeries gone wrong. She found a beautiful vintage map of Galveston that would be perfect for Paul's birthday present.

Dorie felt an urgency to get back to Clementine, but she could never resist the glass display case near the front of the store, which held treasures seemingly not of this world. Inside, she spied a beautiful memento mori, set behind glass within an oval frame. The posy was composed of gray-blonde strands of human hair, intricately knotted and plaited, looped and curled into flora and stem—the only tangible remains of a loved one kept close. She'd wanted to own one of these treasures for a long time.

"May I see that, please?"

The salesclerk, as dusty as the artifacts on the back of the shelves, unlatched the case and handed it to Dorie. "This is an exceptional example—Victorian, of course. They did love their mourning memorabilia. It started with Queen Victoria after she lost her beloved husband, Albert." The words only half registered as Dorie imagined the coiled strands between her fingers, the faint lingering of perfumed hair tonics. "She saved a lock of his hair, which she wore inside a locket. Then artists started creating these beautiful pieces from the hair of lost loved ones to commemorate them."

The clerk reached for a tiny gilded glass vial. "We also have a tear catcher, if you're interested. Mothers and widows collected their tears in these receptacles and saved them until the tears evaporated. That signified their period of mourning was over."

Does a mourning period have a set time frame, an end point that releases us from grieving?

"How much for the memento mori?"

"Five hundred dollars for this one."

Dorie reminded herself that she was living on a fixed budget and needed to watch every penny, so she reluctantly handed it back to the clerk, who seemed relieved not to have to part with it. Dorie had saved a lock of Harriet's hair from her first haircut, not knowing at the time that she should have saved more. Once she'd lost most of her hair from the chemo, it was too late.

Rounding the corner of Avenue B, Dorie almost lost her footing off the steep curb, built for horse and carriages to deposit their passengers onto safe ground. Reflexively, she began to reach out toward a woman in front of her to catch herself. The woman was disheveled, with a tangle of long dark hair, her clothes hanging off her as if she'd recently shrunk.

Dorie managed to regain her balance and pulled back, now noticing that the woman was frantically turning her head left and right, searching the crowd in a panic. Dorie's heart hammered—could it be her?

The woman called out when she finally spied a young girl up ahead and gathered her into her arms. She then immediately proceeded to reprimand her for her wayward ways.

Dorie suddenly felt foolish for thinking it might have been Clementine, that she had run away again. Was she forever cursed to see not only Harriet in every young girl but now Clementine in every young mother as well?

Dorie struggled to open the front door, shopping bags banging against her knees. Clementine was reading in the living room, one hand resting on her book, the other fidgeting with Finn's shell, Rosie asleep on her lap. It took a few moments for her to extract herself from the book, and she looked up as if wondering who this stranger was, entering her house. Then her eyes flicked back to reality as she blinked rapidly.

"I bought you a few things . . . some clothes, toiletries . . ." Dorie tried to sound cheerful as she dropped the bags at Clementine's feet like an offering. "Why don't you take them to your room and try them on? I wasn't sure what size to get. I hope they fit okay."

Clementine stood slowly and gathered the bags, looking somewhat confused, and walked toward the back of the house.

Dorie went back down to the car and took out the painting supplies, which she unpacked in the garage next to the easel. Her stomach fluttered in anticipation, wanting to do something good for Clementine, wanting to reach her.

When she went back upstairs, Clementine was reading again, but she'd changed into the new leggings and blue sweater that Dorie had thought would complement her dark hair. Dorie realized, though, that the clothes weren't right, that Clementine still looked as if she were playing dress up.

Dorie tried to picture how she must have looked when she first met Lou and they'd fallen in love. Or as Curtis's mermaid. She could only have been in her mid to late twenties, but she looked older, her beauty and youth tainted by sorrow and whatever else she'd had to endure over the last few months.

"Clementine, I bought something else for you. It's in the garage." Clementine looked up from the book but stayed seated. "Do you want to come see?" She put the book down and stood, silently following Dorie.

When Dorie opened the garage door, she looked over her shoulder at Clementine, watching for her reaction. Clementine stared at the easel for a minute, as if trying to recall its meaning. Then she turned away and walked back up the stairs.

What on earth's the matter with her? After I went to all that trouble . . .

When Dorie returned upstairs, Clementine was sitting on the couch, clasping and unclasping her hands, fingers fluttering like baby birds attempting to fly. Dorie sat next to her, waiting.

Clementine shifted away slightly. "I can't paint anymore."

"But it might help—"

"I wasn't watching him."

Dorie recalled with alarm the newspaper article she'd read that said the mother had been painting when her son went into the water. Her vision filled with Finn's blue body emerging from the sea, the easel abandoned on the beach nearby.

"That was my job. As his mother. To protect him."

"You were a good mother. We can't always protect those we love."

Clementine turned to look at her, voice accusatory, as if she knew. "How do you know what kind of mother I was?" Dorie's eyes clouded over, and she looked down. *I know because I chose to intrude on your most private thoughts,* Dorie admitted to herself. *And I know only too well how futile it was for us to think we could save either of our children from harm.*

Shaking her head slowly, Clementine continued in a voice firm and hard with self-condemnation. "I failed him. I can't paint again."

danaus

C lementine kept her head down as she followed Dorie along the sand, hair hiding her face, arms dangling loose. They'd been inside for what seemed like weeks, and Dorie had finally coerced her into going for a walk on the beach. She listened to the waves, but no voices called to her now. When she looked up, Dorie was far ahead, waiting for her to catch up.

Clementine noticed something in her peripheral vision—a butterfly. She began to follow it, her eyes fixed. Up ahead, a coarse bush growing by the dunes displayed bright orange-and-black flowers, their petals ablaze in the morning light. Dorie joined her, and as they drew closer, Clementine saw monarch butterflies, like hundreds of miniature stained-glass windows. They returned to Texas in early spring from wintering in Mexico, ready to spawn a new generation. Transfixed, Clementine began to trace her memories.

Every year, Clementine and her father would visit Angangueo to honor her mother. On the mountain top, monarch butterflies would hang from oyamel tree branches, thousands of them, in pleated layers like discarded quince-añera dresses. During Día de los Muertos, families would gather, bringing picnics and sharing stories, memories of their loved ones. She would watch them laugh and weep and dance and eat while her father stood silently by her side. He in his black suit and she in a white dress with ribbons that her *niñera*, Maria, insisted she wear—the perfect little daughter. Her father's grief was a silent and endless prayer between himself and God, a conversation Clementine had never been a part of. So she had waited and watched the butterflies and the families and wondered what it felt like to be loved.

Dorie lightly touched her arm, a connection that drew her back to the present, there by the sea. They stood side by side and peered down at the butterflies, their clockwork wings moving slightly in the breeze.

"In Mexico, many believe butterflies are the souls of loved ones who have died and return to us," Clementine said. Dorie looked at her, and Clementine knew that she too saw Finn and Harriet in their wings.

They walked along the sand again, the butterfly following them. Dorie stayed close to Clementine and shared her story.

"When Harriet was in first grade, her class did a project on monarch butterflies. We bought a bug basket and a milkweed bush that we planted in the garden." Dorie looked up at the butterfly now and again as she continued, a faint smile on her lips. "Harriet checked it every day, looking for eggs."

Clementine imagined the tiny eggs like pearls, hidden in the palms of curled leaves.

"One day, she found the milkweed crawling with monarch caterpillars. Harriet picked her favorite and named it Queenie. She placed it carefully inside the bug basket and added a sprig of milkweed. When she checked an hour or so later, Queenie had devoured it. By the end of the first week, the bush we had planted was stripped bare, and I had to buy two more of them." Dorie laughed softly, a sound Clementine hadn't heard her make before, so that she was unsure of its tilted cadence. "After the third week, Queenie formed her body into a J attached to the top of the basket."

Clementine conjured an image of the chrysalis, a jade finger threaded with gold like a precious jewel. Slowly, it would reveal the inner crush of folded velvet, hints of orange and black within translucent skin.

"Harriet and I watched Queenie emerge from her casing one sunny morning, uncrumpling herself in the warmth of the day. Harriet thought it was magical."

Another butterfly had joined the one hovering between them, as if they were waiting to hear the rest of Dorie's story.

"Harriet watched Queenie test her wings, begging her to stay. Eventually, I convinced her to open the basket door, and Queenie fluttered into the sky, followed by Harriet's pleas for her to return the next spring. And so she did—at least, that's what we told Harriet when the milkweed was once again cluttered with butterflies, and we identified one of them as Queenie."

Dorie finished her story as they crossed the dune closest to the house. One of the butterflies almost brushed Clementine's cheek with its wing before they both rose higher and higher, until they disappeared from view.

"Why can't beautiful things stay?" Clementine asked.

Dorie remained silent, the smile that had lingered on her lips slowly fading.

survival

*d*orie and Clementine's daily walks along the water ful-filled Dorie's constant yearning for sand under her feet, but she still wanted to hear the waves as a constant backdrop. She opened all the windows in the yellow house to let in the warm April breeze, which dispersed the stillness.

Clementine cracked pecans from a platter, one by one, placing the empty shells in a blue bowl in her lap. "I wonder how I learned to love Finn when I was never shown how."

"Oh, we don't learn to love our children. We just do." Dorie arranged mugs and a teapot on the countertop and began spooning tea into the pot from a tin canister, counting under her breath.

"Do we? Not my father. I spent most of my childhood attempting to justify my existence. Survivor's guilt, they call it." She gave a brittle laugh like cracked glass. "I'm good at survival whether I like it or not."

Dorie dropped the spoon onto the counter with a metallic thud. Her voice hardened. "Don't joke about that." She picked it up again and poured the tea back into the canister, having to start over. "We need our instinct to survive just as much as we need our instinct to love. You can't have one without the other."

"But you survived without love."

Dorie's anger dissipated as she spoke softly. "I suppose so. Perhaps survival isn't enough without love."

She went to the fridge and removed milk for herself and a lemon for Clementine. Opening the drawer, she retrieved a knife and started slicing the lemon. A papercut on her finger stung, and the sharp pain momentarily replaced the other deeper one. Dorie brought the tea into the living room, handing a mug to Clementine.

"My mother died when I was born, and my father never really got over it. I think she was the only person he truly loved." Clementine's voice sounded thin in the early spring air that entered from the open window. "I found some letters, once, that he'd written to her. I couldn't believe my father had written those words, that he was capable of love like that."

Dorie chewed a nut that Clementine handed her, the bitter dryness coating her tongue.

"I tried to make him love me. Studied hard, read a lot. . . . But whatever I did was never enough for him, so I quit trying. He sent me away to boarding school after that." Clementine picked up a throw from the chair and wrapped it around herself. "By the end of high school, I spent most of my time in the art studio. Painting, writing, screwing my teacher." Dorie frowned. "He wasn't that much older than me."

"Well, that's beside the point. He was your *teacher.*"

Clementine shrugged off her disapproval. "Part of the thrill was hoping my father would find out, but he never did. Why would he? I was invisible to him."

"He was likely grieving, for your mother," said Dorie. "We both know the damage grief can do."

"But I was his only child. I was all he had." Clementine's dark eyes flashed. "When I graduated, I skipped town before the ceremony. My father wasn't coming anyway." She said it matter-of-factly, as though it were nothing. "And when I met Lou and got pregnant with Finn a few months later, that was the last straw, as far as my father was concerned."

"But surely, given the circumstances . . ."

"No. I don't talk to my father." Clementine reached for Finn's shell, where it sat at the base of her throat. "He never forgave me for my mother's death, and I'll never forgive myself for Finn's." She picked at the fringe on the blanket, separating the twisted strands with her fingers, so that tufts of yellow fiber fell to the floor.

"It wasn't your fault, Clementine. It was an accident. These tragedies are out of our hands."

"Like Harriet's cancer?"

Dorie's face shifted. "I blamed myself for not doing enough for a long time. Perhaps I still do . . ."

"You haven't forgiven yourself either."

Dorie took her hand. "Let's at least offer absolution to each other. It's a start."

Clementine nodded. "I think I can do that."

my darlin' clementine

Clementine continued sipping from her mug of tea, the yellow fiber from the throw blanket scattering like petals from a wilted flower.

"What about Finn's father? Were you happy with him?" Dorie asked tentatively.

"The beginning was magical, as I suppose beginnings are," Clementine said. "It just didn't last . . ."

Clementine dreaded her shift; she'd worked way too much in the past two weeks and was exhausted. She never got good tips when she was tired.

"Another round, darlin'!"

Clementine forced a wide smile. "Coming right up." She swerved out of reach as one of them attempted to swat her ass.

When the table finally closed up for the night, one of them handed her a fifty. "For your smile." She took it because she needed the money, but she wished she'd tossed it back in his face.

Two days later, she had just finished the lunch shift and was dying to get home. Her latest painting was almost done, and she wanted to work on it before her crazy roommate, Stacey, showed up and bombarded her with her latest drama. The streets of Montrose had emptied some as diners returned to work, so she walked quickly down the sidewalk, dodging roots that broke through the ground like arthritic knuckles.

"Hi, Clementine. Remember me?"

She looked up at the man in front of her, who seemed to take up too much space. Her breath quickened.

"I tipped you the—"

"Right. And what do you imagine that will get you?"

"Lunch, maybe?" He shrugged and pulled out a cigarette. Inhaling deeply, he watched her face through a veil of smoke. Then he held the open pack of cigarettes toward her.

"No thanks. I don't."

"What? Eat lunch?"

She struggled to hold his gaze, refusing to reveal her discomfort at being examined. Refusing to reveal the rush in her veins like an electrical surge through a wire.

"I'm Lou, in case you forgot. Listen, I want to apologize for my buddies' behavior the other night. I was celebrating, and I guess we got kind of carried away."

"I see a lot of that."

"I want to make it up to you. Let me take you to lunch."

"I already ate." She started to walk down the street.

"How about tonight, then? Dinner?"

"Sorry, I have plans tonight."

"Damn. Well, okay. Another time, then," Lou called after her as she walked away.

The heat from the day lingered, mixing with the soupy humidity and making it impossible not to sweat within five minutes of leaving the apartment. Clementine's roommate was getting over a broken heart, and the best way she knew to do that was to get wasted at their favorite bar and sleep with someone as quickly as possible.

Stacey scanned the place for a possible candidate, avoiding eye contact with men who didn't qualify. "What about him?" Stacey suggested, directing her eyes toward a large, dark man holding a beer and smoking a cigarette.

Shit! "No, he looks like trouble to me."

"I like a bit of trouble. I'm not looking for Mr. Right, remember?"

Lou noticed them checking him out and walked over. "Well, fancy running into you here."

"You know each other?" Stacey asked.

"Not yet," Lou said with one of his disarming smiles. That's when Clementine knew she'd go home with him.

Stacey whispered into Clementine's ear, "You better go for that, girl, or I will. Whether he likes it or not!"

Clementine woke the following morning tangled up with Lou in his unwashed sheets that smelled of cedarwood left in the rain. Pale light shone through the shutters, striping his bare skin light and dark. He breathed loudly, and Clementine felt his heat on the back of her neck. Her head throbbed, and her mouth screamed for water.

She rehashed the evening as best she could. Stacey had quickly ditched them for a boyish blond frat boy. "Totally not my type. Perfect!" she'd announced as she presented him with yet another beer and sidled close. Clementine and Lou had danced to some slow, sad song that made her forget who she was, and Lou laughed like a man wandering and almost happy.

Clementine woke again later to the smell of bacon and coffee. A glass of water sat next to the bed with two aspirin close by, which she gulped down. When she trudged into the kitchen, Lou was busy at the stove, wearing only torn-up jeans and humming. Her blood hummed along with him.

"Morning, darlin'. Hungry?"

"Why are you always trying to feed me?"

"I like feeding people. And I do it pretty well, or so I've been told."

"Huh. Is that your version of seduction, then?"

"Well, hopefully just one of them."

Lou grinned at her, and she remembered his tongue against her skin the night before. Clementine looked away from him abruptly and down at the plate in front of her. She took a bite from some sort of egg concoction that tasted as good as it smelled.

"How did you learn to cook like this?"

"Cooking for my brothers and sisters. They liked eating better when it tasted good, so I learned to cook. I worked in restaurant kitchens to help make ends meet after my dad ran out on my mom."

"I don't cook, can barely boil an egg."

"You didn't ever cook with your family?"

"I didn't really have a family, as such."

"Everyone has a family."

"Not true."

Lou's smile faltered for a moment, but Clementine kept eating and his face lit up again as he watched her relish his food. "The guys on the rig appreciate my cooking too. Helps with morale when things get lonely out there—a good home-cooked meal, like Mama used to make." Lou joined her at the table but mostly just watched her eat. "What about you? What do you do, besides waitressing?"

"I paint."

"What, like houses?"

"No, like pictures."

"Huh. Pictures of what?"

"All sorts of things. People, mostly. You'll have to see for yourself."

"Is that an invitation?"

"I think so," she said.

"So when can I see them?"

"Do you always move this fast?"

"No."

"Well, neither do I, so we'll see, okay? Right now, I need to get home and shower and head to work."

And that's how the next few months went. Him, cooking and laughing and loving. Her, absorbing his attentions while wondering when it would change.

And it did change. They quickly found themselves skipping nights out at crowded bars. She'd drag him to art museums, and he'd take her to his favorite Vietnamese restaurants, where no one spoke English and they pointed to what they wanted on the menu. Or they'd spend their time just enjoying each other at home. Then, before she could talk herself out of it, they rented the little yellow house by the sea.

the lighthouse

*d*orie was putting away clean laundry, grumbling about having to do all the work herself. But though the weight of Clementine's trauma seemed to have settled into a low hum over the weeks she'd been there, it still reverberated at certain moments, so Dorie felt uneasy asking Clementine to help with chores.

Later, when she feels better. Though I suppose then she'll move on. Won't she?

Dorie opened a dresser drawer in the bedroom to drop in a pile of clean socks and was surprised to find the watercolor of the sailboat that had hung on the wall. It lay facedown. She picked it up and looked at it more closely. *CC* was written in the lower right corner of the painting.

So Clementine painted it before leaving the house. Perhaps for Finn.

Dorie supposed it served as a reminder of Clementine's self-imposed vow not to paint again. She wondered if Clementine still wrote, though she'd seen no evidence of it. Dorie hadn't read Clementine's journal since she'd moved in two months ago. Their face-to-face conversations had replaced the words on the page.

Which words are truer?

"Are you sure you don't want to come with me?" Dorie asked, uncomfortable about leaving Clementine alone again. Clementine shook her head and continued reading. Lynn had invited them both to dinner, and Dorie was especially excited because her friend had promised to show her around the lighthouse.

Dorie took a shower and, by five, was ready and sitting in a chair, trying to read. Rennie was supposed to be picking her up at five thirty, which probably meant six. She went to the kitchen for water and caught her reflection in the mirror. The yellow dress she wore made her too-pale skin sallow, as if she were recovering from a long illness.

Dorie went back to the closet and stared at the racks of clothes arranged before her, feeling overwhelmed. She quickly changed into the blue dress she'd tried on earlier and scrutinized herself in the mirror—still slim, but looser, her curves softer, even with all her walking.

"Clementine?" Dorie knocked on her bedroom door.

"Yes."

"Is this better than the yellow?"

Clementine dragged her eyes from the book she was reading and stared at Dorie blankly. "The yellow?"

"Never mind." She turned around and closed the door, smoothing her dress and taking a deep breath. Her eyes darted over to the clock: five forty-five. She vowed not to check it again.

Five minutes later, slow footsteps sounded on the stairs, and she opened the front door before Rennie had time to knock, purse in hand. He chuckled. "I guess you're ready to go, huh?" Rennie walked her to the passenger side of his truck and held the door open, unsuccessful in hiding his suppressed grin. Dorie chided herself, knowing she needed to relax and give in to beach time.

Once they got on the road, Rennie turned up the radio and tapped the steering wheel in rhythm to the music. Tilting electrical poles flicked by, looking like they could topple over at any moment. Birds perched daintily on the wires, tails tipping as they tried to keep their balance. Dorie forced her shoulders to relax and looked over at Rennie.

"How long has Lynn owned the lighthouse?" She imagined circular rooms spiraling upward to the top of the tower, furniture designed to tuck into curves and secret nooks.

Glancing at her, Rennie turned the radio back down. "Lynn and Ken inherited it from her grandparents. It had been vacant for years until they bought it—in '47, I believe."

They arrived then, as if on cue, pulling into a lot where the lighthouse towered to the left of them, incongruous next to three smaller cottages. The Bolivar Lighthouse wasn't one featured on a calendar, painted a bright white, or decorated with red stripes and surrounded by flowers. It stood tall and skinny, clad in rusty black iron, a brittle old lady wearing her faded Sunday best.

The truck door screeched off-key when Dorie opened it, Rennie not quite getting to her side in time, so that he hovered awkwardly as she got out of the truck. They made their way to one of the houses, its weathered siding faded to a denim blue and contrasting with the bright-red front door.

When Rennie knocked, there was no response, so he walked around the side of the house. Dorie followed, keeping to the flagstone path that led through patches of orange cosmos, pink evening primrose, and moss verbena. A large

raised bed contained various herbs—lemon mint, basil, rosemary—and a number of vegetables, in the middle of which
lounged a fat tabby lazily licking her paws.

Music came from the house, and when they reached the
back door, Dorie spied Lynn and her husband two-stepping
around the kitchen island. He dipped her as the last note
played, and her long blonde hair brushed the floor.

Rennie knocked again and then pushed the back door
open. "Howdy. It's just us. Sorry to interrupt!"

"You're here! Feel like joining in?" Lynn took Rennie's
hand and did a graceful twirl under his arm.

Her husband laughed as he held out his hand to Dorie.
"Hi, I'm Ken. You must be Dorie." He was a tall, handsome
man wearing a gingham apron over jeans that were tucked
into snakeskin cowboy boots. Dorie quickly released his hand,
just in case he attempted a dance move. "Let's get you a drink.
Wine, beer, or sweet tea?" He held up a bottle of white wine.

"Wine would be nice."

Ken poured a generous glass, which he handed to Dorie,
and Lynn held out her almost empty one for a refill. Rennie
helped himself to a longneck from the fridge.

"Cheers!" Lynn clinked her glass against Dorie's, followed by Ken and Rennie. Dorie took a long swallow of the
cold sweet wine. She looked out the window at the lighthouse,
silhouetted against the fading sky. Austere and rigid.

Impenetrable.

"How's life treating you, buddy?" Ken asked, turning to
Rennie.

Lynn scooped her long hair up into a bundle and clipped
it messily into place. "Come on, Dorie. We'll leave them to it.
Let's start with the star of the show."

Dorie followed Lynn outside. "I can't imagine what it
must be like to own a lighthouse."

"It's funny, but we don't really think of it as *our* lighthouse. It seems to belong to the past, to previous generations. You'll feel it when you're in there." They made their way to the back door. "Let me tell you, though, it can get kind of spooky sometimes, especially after a big storm."

The lighthouse almost looked less imposing up close, where Dorie could see the battle scars and neglect. She placed her hand on the wall of the tower, trying to envision it during its heyday. A sentinel, invisible in the dark, except for the roaming beam of light that searched the fog for lost ships.

Lynn opened the heavy iron door, which let out a painful groan. "We're pretty close to being done with the house, but this beauty needs some big-time attention."

Dorie was surprised by the expansive lower level. Brick-masonry walls revealed several openings into other rooms, which stood empty apart from a bleached bird skeleton, picked clean, among bird droppings that lay claim to the space. As they started climbing the steep spiral staircase, she inhaled the salty-rusty air and remarked on how narrow the tower became as they got higher.

"Believe it or not, during the Great Storm of 1900, it sheltered over 120 people from the storm," Lynn said. They arrived at the top of the stairs and walked out onto the deck, where the wind whipped through the glassless windows. "After the floodwater receded, they found a dozen bodies outside, people who weren't able to reach the tower in time."

Dorie ran her fingers over the pitted skin of the cool iron walls, pushing away an image of Clementine clutching Finn's blue body—suddenly wanting to rush home.

a salve and a blade

*C*lementine opened the windows so she could hear the waves. The voices had abandoned her. Or perhaps she had abandoned them. Chilled by the artificial air churned out by the AC, she searched for socks. She uncovered Finn's sailboat painting, which she'd hidden in the drawer, the only remnant besides memories and ghosts.

And Tabitha, who was outside, chasing sunlight and crickets in the yard. She refused to call her Rosie; she was still Clementine's cat. Even though it sometimes hurt to look at her and remember her squirming body in Finn's clumsy embrace.

She brushed her hand against the pine walls as she left the bedroom. With Dorie gone, it felt a little more like her house again. But Dorie would be home soon, and Clementine would once again have to relinquish it to her.

The table where she had sat with Finn and Lou was still there, though. She felt them in her bones, images flickering like home movies: Lou and Finn constructing a fort out of bedsheets held up by these very kitchen chairs; Finn begging her not to dismantle it, even though the house resembled a war zone; making a fire on the beach one night, by which she and Finn danced for Lou, their shadows mimicking them among the sparks.

The images faded to white. Her memories were both a salve and a blade that reopened her wounds.

Clementine went to the bookcase, where the photo of Harriet was tucked between the wall of books. Her eye caught on an object as intimate as her own hand. She reached for it, her fingers wrapping around the leather cover. Her words spilled out from its pages . . .

August 3, 2003

Today, I was working on a painting, and Finn was at his easel as well. I got lost in my work and didn't realize he'd wandered off. Must have been ten minutes or so. I panicked that he'd gone to the water, but I found him because of the racket. He was crouched in the outdoor shower, absorbed in his task: collecting frogs in his red bucket! They congregate there after the rain. Must have been twenty or so piled in that bucket, clambering all over each other. He looked up at me with a dazed look, then his face broke out into a smile. He held out his pail of frogs: Look, Mama! I saved them!

The words mocked her: *Remember when you used to laugh at your overprotectiveness of the child, your most precious possession? And then you lost him.* She tightened her other hand into a fist so her nails marked the skin in half moons. *Even he was capable of saving a living creature. But not you. His mother. It could so easily have happened that time. And so many others. You should have known he wasn't safe. You should have been more careful. And now he's gone. There's nothing left of him.*

Because of you.

There were markings in the margins—question marks and stars—not of her own making. *Did Dorie do this? Does she also have the rest of my things, my drawings and paintings, hidden away somewhere like stolen treasure?*

Clementine reached for a pencil on the desk and turned to a blank page in the journal. She scratched at its surface until Finn's face emerged from the gray lines. But not his eyes. She tore the page free and started again. And again. Over and over. Until his face disappeared from her mind and she was left with nothing but a shifting memory that faded until it had receded into the dark.

eclipse

*d*orie looked around the dining room that glowed a pinkish-golden hue from the setting sun, which crept through the lace curtains that adorned the abundance of tall sash windows. The large dining table was piled with platters of fragrant gumbo, fresh shrimp, steaming rolls, and an enormous salad. Dorie took a bite of the greens, which hinted at the soil they had grown from. Ken attributed it to his wife's green thumb, bragging about how she'd won best in show for the last five years for her homegrown vegetables.

Beadboard walls displayed paintings and photos, one of which was a sepia photograph of two grim-looking men. "They were quite a pair," said Lynn. "It's rumored that one of them would flash passing trains!" The image made Dorie blush, and Lynn laughed loudly. "Not a pretty picture, however you look at it!"

Dorie attempted to change the subject. "There were trains here at one time?"

"The old railroad ran just outside the fence on the south side, between the lighthouse and the highway. The rails and ties were picked up long ago, but you can still see where they were."

Dorie thought of all the hidden pieces of Bolivar's past that emerged from the land and water, restive spirits unwilling to leave the world of the living.

Lynn pointed to another image on the wall. "And that's a painting my cousin did of a keeper who was considered the best in the district. Served for twenty-four years."

Dorie admired the brushstrokes that had captured an honest heart in a stern face, the lines etched like crevices in stone, softened only by an abundance of white whiskers. But his eyes were a soft brown, and faint wrinkles, like unironed silk, crinkled the outer edges.

"Here, you must try the gumbo," Lynn insisted, passing a bowl to Dorie. "It's Ken's specialty."

Dorie set the bowl down, her mouth watering as steam rose from it. Then Rennie handed her an overflowing platter of shrimp. Dorie popped one into her mouth. It tasted of the sea.

"Rennie and Ken caught those this morning with Pete, so they're super fresh," Lynn boasted, rubbing Ken's arm affectionately.

"Isn't Pete the shrimp guy that Lou's staying with?" Dorie asked.

"Yep," Rennie said. "He's right off Madison, near Port Bolivar, close by here. Matter of fact, Lou came out with us on the boat today."

Lynn asked Dorie if Clementine knew that Lou was on the peninsula. "I haven't told her," said Dorie. She was struggling between the fear of upsetting Clementine and the need to warn her in case he appeared again. "Though I'm surprised he hasn't found out about her yet." *Especially considering Lynn's apparent penchant for gossip.*

"Maybe you should tell her," said Lynn. "It could be quite the scene if he confronts her out of the blue."

Again, Dorie fought the urge to make her excuses and rush back home to check on Clementine. Lynn seemed to sense her unease and turned her attention to Rennie.

"How's Carl doing? Is he enjoying being back on the road?"

Rennie slowly shook his head. "I'm sure he is. Not so sure I like it too much, though. Last time I spoke to him, he was sleeping in the van. Not making enough money for a room. Won't let me lend him any."

"He'll be fine," said Ken. "It's good for him to live rough for a while. Toughen him up."

Dorie watched Rennie try to smile, recognizing the effort. If it were up to her, no one would suffer in order to be strong.

"Hey, Rennie, I have a proposition for you," said Ken. Rennie looked down, as if he knew what was coming and didn't much like it. "A friend of mine on the mainland wants to build a house on some land he owns here. Beachfront property. You interested?" Ken leaned forward, eyes bright.

Rennie shook his head. "I've told you over and over, Ken, I don't do that anymore."

"But he's a good buddy of mine, and he knows your work. He really wants you to build his house. Could you consider it as a favor? Just this one time?"

Dorie interrupted, "Those other two cottages—what do you use them for?"

As Lynn began to explain, Rennie looked relieved and gave Dorie a subtle nod of thanks for changing the subject.

"So this is the keeper's cottage." Lynn then pointed to the larger of the two other cottages through the window. "That one there was where the assistant keeper lived, and the other was the radio shack for the lighthouse. We haven't done much with those two yet. They're on the endless to-do list."

They continued talking until napkins littered the table and their glasses sat almost empty.

"We'll clean up," said Rennie. "You ladies go relax."

Lynn gave him a quick peck on the cheek. "You're an angel in disguise."

Lynn and Dorie went outside to sit on the front porch and enjoy their coffee in the buzzing warmth of the May evening.

"Rennie's such a great guy, isn't he?" said Lynn. "I don't know what Shel would do without him. He's helped raise her kids since their daddy left. I worried about him when he came back from Louisiana after he and his wife, Claire, split. He just wasn't himself. He's always been such a sweet, laid-back guy, but I think he was angry at Claire and missed Carl."

"So Carl stayed with his mom?"

"For a while, but he and Rennie stayed close. Rennie would visit him in Louisiana every month or so, and then Carl would spend summers here. I think he would have preferred to stay with Rennie, really. He came to live with him right out of high school and has stayed here since."

The clatter of dishes came from the kitchen, mixed with deep laughter and music from the radio. "He's certainly got something," Dorie said, remembering how Carl had shone up on stage.

"He gets his good looks and charisma from his father. Not so much the singing, mind you. I suppose I have to give some credit to Claire for that. It's hard for Rennie to see him go, though. He worries about him and has gotten used to having him around, as we all have. Still, now he has you." Lynn paused her chattering and turned to look at Dorie.

"Me?" She took a sip of coffee, scalding her tongue as she swallowed.

"Well, yes. I mean a new friend, to distract him from being lonely. We can all use new friends, right?"

Dorie imagined Rennie was the last person who needed more friends. He was probably the least lonely person she'd ever met. But she did want to be his friend; he made the world a nicer place. Dorie registered Lynn's look—anticipating her response, reading her expression. Dorie worried about what Lynn might have seen.

"He's certainly been helpful with Clementine and Lou."

"He wants to help. We all do. How *is* Clementine? It must be difficult having her stay with you. I'm not sure I could handle it."

"She's a little better, has opened up to me a bit." Dorie wondered if Lynn knew of their connection, formed through their shared loss and grief. If Rennie had told her about Harriet.

Footsteps clomped over the wooden floor of the deck. "Okay, we're done. Time for a nightcap before we head back," Rennie said as both men joined them, glasses clinking.

Drowsy from the wine, Dorie sat quietly, fading into the background as she observed the camaraderie between the three friends. The lighthouse had almost disappeared in the dark, but the three surrounding cottages blazed with light. An eclipse of moths fluttered around the light above her, their tattered gray wings like wraiths.

"You ready, Dorie? You look like you're about to drop off."

Rennie stood and turned to his friends. "We should probably head back. Thank you both for the feast and the hospitality." He hugged them, and Dorie stood, a little unsteadily. Thanking her hosts, she accepted Lynn's hug and kiss on the cheek and Ken's warm handshake.

They made their way back to the truck, Rennie holding her elbow as they navigated the flagstone path. The pressure of his hand was like heat soothing a sore muscle.

On the ride home, Dorie rolled down her window, hoping the cool night air would clear her head a little.

"So, was the lighthouse what you expected?" asked Rennie.

"I actually didn't quite know what to expect. But it's beautiful." Dorie watched Rennie's hands, where they rested on the steering wheel. A working man's hands. "Lynn and Ken are nice." She imagined herself laughing easily with the three of them, dancing with Rennie like Lynn had with Ken, drinking too much wine and eating shrimp caught that very day.

"Yep, they're good folks."

"How long is Carl away on tour?"

"He left a couple of weeks ago. No idea when he'll be back."

"You must miss him."

"I do. He's done this before, but only nearby—Houston, Austin. This time, he's traveling to several cities across the US; he'll be gone a good while, I expect." Rennie paused, and Dorie felt Carl's absence. "But he needs this. Either to find out he can make a living with his own music or to realize he can't and settle down somewhere, find something else to love."

The scent of aged leather upholstery made her wonder what Rennie smelled like. She shifted in her seat, a fraction closer. They pulled up the track to her house, and Rennie put the truck in park, the engine idling. Mosquitoes swarmed in, so he shut the windows and turned on the AC. Dorie reached for the door.

"Thanks for inviting me tonight. It was nice."

Rennie looked at her hand where it rested on the chrome handle. "It was. And you're very welcome."

She began to tremble. *Must be the cold air in the truck.* She pushed open the door, letting the warmth and mosquitoes rush in again, but still her body vibrated. Rennie smiled and looked away as she got out and closed the truck door, lingering for just a moment. Then she started to walk slowly toward the stairs of her yellow house, imagining sitting at the top of a tall tower, watching the dark water for lost ships.

Guiding them home.

released

*d*igging through the nearby desk, Clementine pulled out bills, notes, letters—searching for Finn's face. Envelopes with her name on them scattered at her feet.

Lou's letters.

She stuffed them into her pocket and continued her search—rushing to closets, emptying boxes, shelves, drawers, cabinets. The attic cord dangled in front of her, grayed by age, frayed at the end. She pulled and unfolded the stairs, which wobbled and shifted under her weight as if they might collapse. Entering the dimness, her eyes strained to adjust.

No paintings leaned against the dusty rafters. Only a solitary cardboard box.

Tearing it open, she found layers of drawings. Narrowing her eyes, she willed herself to see. *No use.* She shifted the box, pushed it forward, leaving a mark on the ashy floor. Then she shoved it through the attic opening and onto the ground, where it landed with a dead thud. The cardboard split on one side, expelling a pink stuffed rabbit, a doll with yellow hair, a sheaf of drawings spilling onto the floor below.

She clambered down too quickly and fell the last few steps, scraping open her knee. Blood smeared one drawing red as she kneeled—a black dog, tongue lolling, sitting under a lollipop-shaped tree.

A child's hand did these. Finn's? No—the name penned carefully on the corner is Harriet. Dorie's dead daughter.

Clementine crumpled the drawing in her hand, tossed it aside. Picked up another. Not hers. Not Finn's. Frantically, she pushed aside pages, crushed and wadded. Nothing. Nothing left of his beautiful face, his boy scent, his once-laughing eyes. Her journal, filled with useless words, sat half buried under the pieces of Harriet that littered the floor.

Harriet, whom she'd released from the dark.

carnage

*d*orie opened the front door with Rosie at her heels, meowing for dinner. Suddenly, her senses, lulled by the wine, were acutely revived as she found Clementine sitting among a carnage of paper. Dorie gasped, and Clementine looked up, her eyes glazed, lost in a faraway place. She clutched her journal to her chest, and Dorie fought an impulse to reach for it. Then Dorie scanned the room and saw a cardboard box split open, Harriet's name written on the outside.

"What have you done?" She reached for a piece of paper at her feet—a drawing of her family standing in a line, the sun shining above them, Harriet's stick fingers reaching for her parents' hands, all smiles.

"You were examining me, studying me." Clementine brandished the journal like a weapon. "Your own life is so empty, you have to slip into mine like you do so many others, inhabiting them so you can ignore your own self."

Dorie looked up at her, breath shallow and fast. "You have no life. You left it all behind, remember?"

Clementine stood and faced her. "So did you! Hiding your daughter in the dark. Pretending she never existed!"

Dorie's jaw set firmly. "She exists for me every single day."

"Then why do you hide her away? Like my drawings and paintings? Where did you hide them?"

Dorie picked up another crumpled drawing and smoothed it with shaking hands, not hearing.

"I need to see him! Where is he?"

"Who?"

"Finn. There was a sketch. Where is it?"

Dorie's chest heaved as she pushed Clementine aside to gather the remains of Harriet. Clementine grabbed her arms, shook her so she was forced to listen.

"What did you do with it?"

Dorie couldn't make sense of what was happening. "Why have you done this?"

Clementine released her and looked around the room, her voice quiet suddenly. "You have all this. What do I have?"

Dorie looked at the ruined remains. "You have nothing. We both have nothing." Hot tears pricked.

Clementine slumped into a chair, and Dorie felt heat rising—she didn't want her sitting there. Didn't want her anywhere near.

"You can't be here."

"I'm not leaving until you give me my things." She said it calmly without looking at Dorie.

Dorie spoke, her voice high, stretched tight with wanting her gone. "I don't have them. Go ask your deadbeat boyfriend where your stuff is."

Clementine stiffened. "Lou?"

"He's here."

"But why? How?"

"Ask *him*."

161

"Why didn't you tell me?"

Dorie couldn't look at her anymore, just wanted her gone. "I'm telling you now. He's in Port Bolivar, Pete's Bait and Tackle shop."

Clementine stood and looked at Dorie with an expression she couldn't read. Then she reached down, scooped Rosie into her arms, and headed to the front door.

"You're not taking her," said Dorie.

"She's my cat."

"Not anymore. You abandoned her, just like you abandoned the rest of your life."

Clementine ignored her and opened the door. Dorie rushed forward and struggled to pull Rosie from her grasp as the cat wailed in alarm, scratching at their hands. They both let go at once, and Rosie darted through the open door.

"Rosie, come back! Rosie!" Dorie cried as she pushed Clementine aside and raced down the wooden steps. She just spotted the white tip of Rosie's tail as she disappeared over the dunes. Clementine ran past in the direction of the road, and Dorie froze, her eyes boring into Clementine's back, willing her away into the dark.

Inside, Dorie gathered Harriet's belongings into a pile and continued trying to salvage what she could of Harriet's drawings, gently smoothing out the pages. They were mostly horses and Daisy, their black lab. Red smeared several images, and Dorie realized it was blood. She couldn't recall Clementine being injured, but she hoped she was—just a little.

Perhaps I can tape some of the drawings back together, make them whole again. Some, she'd have to throw away, as they were beyond repair. And it broke her heart.

It was two in the morning when Dorie finally went to bed, her mind drifting to the edges of sleep. She dreamed of searching through cupboards piled with cracked china patterned with seashells and red coral, with stacks of maritime oil paintings depicting grizzled sea captains and hulking ships. She turned each dream object over in her hands, appreciating the gifts the house offered.

Then her search became more frantic. She dug through endless heaps of shells, tossed aside tackle boxes brimming with used lures, their rusted hooks puncturing her skin. Stacks of books and scribbled pages grew around her, drowning her in words she was unable to decipher. Stick-fingered hands reached for her, gripped tighter and tighter, so that her bones cracked.

Until they released her, broken but free.

fragments

even at this time of night, cars sped past Clementine as she walked, headlights slicing the darkness. Cars shrieked and snarled so that she stumbled and swerved into the road. It felt as if she'd walked for miles when a car pulled over, its red signal light blinking on and off like a warning.

The driver rolled down his window. "Need a ride?" Clementine opened the door and got in. The car smelled of sweat and potato chips. A life gone wrong. "Where you headed?"

"Port Bolivar," she said, with a certainty that caught her off guard.

"You catching the ferry? I'm going that way myself."

Clementine felt him looking too hard. "No, but close by." She touched Finn's shell. She'd reknotted the fraying string so many times, it was getting tight around her throat.

He pulled onto the road again. "What you doing out walking so late?" He looked over at her. "Get in a fight with a boyfriend or something?" The black pressed down so she could hardly breathe. He grunted and stared straight ahead.

"Not very friendly, are you? No wonder your boyfriend ditched you." He shuffled a bit in his seat before continuing in a low, gravelly voice. "Still, I'm happy to lend a helping hand to someone in need . . . are you in need?" His palm was damp on her knee. She clenched her teeth to stop their chattering as his fingers kneaded her thigh.

When the lighthouse loomed to their right, she knew they were close. He turned off the highway, and she tried to read the street signs.

"Where's your place, then?"

That's when she saw it: *Pete's Bait and Tackle. Fresh Shrimp For Sale.* "Right there."

He pulled over and turned off the engine, whispering through the dark. "Hey, why don't I come in for a nightcap? As a thank you, for helping you out tonight."

He leaned over, and she smelled his breath, fumbling lust turned to hate. Clementine reached for the door handle behind her and flung open the car door. His fingers gripped her arm, trying to pull her back. Then she bit down, her teeth tearing until she tasted blood.

"Goddamn bitch! Get the fuck off me!"

He released her, and she ran toward the sign, ran up the dirt track to the house. Pounding on the front door, blinded by fear and rage. The blood-metal taste lingered in her mouth, reminding her of what dying might feel like.

Muffled footsteps sounded behind the door. "Jesus— I'm coming. What the fuck time is it?" When the door opened, he stepped back.

It's not him. Another man, blurred with sleep. "Lou. I need to see Lou." She panted and wiped her mouth, red smearing her hand. Clementine looked behind her for the man in the car. An engine started up and growled away into the night.

When she looked back at the doorway, the man was

watching her carefully. He stayed quiet, just nodded once. She followed him around to the back of the house, where he gestured to a decrepit trailer partially hidden by an overgrown tangle of brush.

Clementine knocked once. When Lou opened the door, his face was a mosaic of jagged corners and distorted lines. He clung to the doorframe as if it could support his bulk and stop him from reaching for her.

"Clementine—"

She forced her way past, trying not to look at him, her eyes darting frantically around the suffocating space, looking for her sketch of Finn. It was taped to the wall next to Lou's bed. Clementine's legs gave way beneath her. She hung onto the bed frame and sat clumsily, Lou's scent rising from the crumpled bedding. Pulling the drawing off the wall, she tore a corner, and Finn was made incomplete.

"Where are the rest?"

"The rest?"

"My drawings, paintings, everything."

"I don't know," Lou whispered, looking away from her.

She held the torn sketch of their son to her chest as she folded her arms around herself, focusing on the frayed hem of her tee shirt.

Lou took a step toward her. "Where have you been?" He bent over, shoulders hunched, head low, trying to reach her eyes with his. "Clem, I can't imagine what you've been going through."

"No, you can't."

Lou straightened. The air in the room turned viscous, his words cumbersome. "He was my son too." She examined her hands clasped tightly in her lap, noticed the raw edges of her fingernails for the first time. "You should have told me. I had to hear about it from the warden." His voice was sharp, like flint.

"You weren't a part of our lives anymore."

Lou sat in the chair opposite her, rubbing his hands up and down the arms. He took a deep breath, gripping tightly, as if forcing his hands to stillness. "That's not true. I deserved to know my son had died. I should have been here. I would've come."

"You were in jail. You couldn't have come," she said, her voice like nails.

"You still should have told me. You could've called, written."

I couldn't have—that blurred sadness emptied me until nothing was left. The room went silent as the AC window unit cut off.

"I know you didn't think I could be a father to him, but I loved him."

She only blinked rapidly and pulled her legs up onto the bed, tucking them beneath her so she resembled a discarded doll, whose limbs were twisted and broken.

"Did you get my letter? About what happened?"

"I stopped reading your letters a long time ago."

"I guess that explains why I quit hearing from you."

"Anyway, I know what happened. You almost killed somebody."

Lou looked down, raked his hand through his hair and closed his eyes.

"It doesn't matter. You weren't a father to him or a partner to me. You were—"

"I was what? A loser? A drunk? An asshole!"

She raised her head and allowed herself to look at him for the first time, his damaged beauty like cracked glass distorting the light. Clementine stood up and walked to the window, turning her back on him, not wanting to see the anger mixed with desperation that made her pity him.

"I know. I wasn't good enough for you." He paused and took a deep breath. The shifting clouds released a shaft of moonlight across the bed for just a moment. "I made a mistake."

She looked back at him then, trying to imagine this man she'd loved spending months in a prison cell while their son lived and then died.

"I had a lot of time to think about how I want to live the rest of my life. And one of the things I figured out is that I want to spend it with you. I never stopped loving you."

"It's too late for us."

"But we can help each other—we need each other."

"I don't need you." She watched the ruin her words inflicted.

Lou moved slowly to the window and put his hand on her shoulder. She smelled his cedar skin and fought against the impulse to touch his hair, a tether forcing her to stillness. "I know losing Finn was the worst thing that could have happened. Believe me, I do know that."

She pulled away from him. "You didn't even know him." She looked into Lou's splintered face, and they stood silently, waiting for the other to mend the fragments.

"I have to go."

"You can't just leave."

Her sketch of Finn was on the bedside table. She picked it up and stood.

"Clem, I'm not giving up on us."

"You need to."

"Well, I'm not. So you take as long as you need. I'll be around. I'm not going anywhere this time." Lou looked at the sketch in her hand. "Please, Clem, let me keep it."

"No, I need to see his face."

Lou paused, then went over to the dining table and dug something out of his wallet. He handed it to Clementine. Finn's shining face grinned back at her, his body leaning into hers. She shone too, so that she didn't recognize herself.

"I'll make you a deal," said Lou softly. "You keep the photo and let me have the drawing. Please."

"You're in no position to make deals with me about my son."

"Our son, Clem."

She looked at the sketch and then at the photograph. Finn's eyes filled with life. She handed Lou the drawing, then walked toward the door. "Where are you going?" He stood in front of her. "I'll take you."

Clementine thought of the yellow house by the water, her home that no longer belonged to her. She couldn't look into Lou's eyes, so she stared straight ahead, concentrating on the blue lines of his shirt. A gold cross nestled in the hollow of his throat.

She knew where to go.

It wasn't far. When Clementine got out of Lou's car and told him to leave, he wouldn't look at her, and she felt his anger, palpable, an old acquaintance that was strangely comforting. Like a pair of old shoes grown tight and stiff, but which she still insisted she could wear. He drove away reluctantly, though she saw his brake lights at the gate as he waited for the front door to open.

Despite the late hour, she lifted the familiar anchor-shaped knocker. It took a few minutes before Earle opened the front door of the white house. He looked at her as if maybe she wasn't really there. Clementine stood before him, not sure whether he was angry or scared. Then he leaned in and wrapped his arms around her, and for the first time since losing Finn, she felt safe.

Inside, Agnes took her hand, her face radiant. "Clementine, we've been waiting for you. The good Lord has answered our prayers."

Clementine struggled to accept her words. Part of her wanted to shout and push Agnes away, to reject her along with her absurd faith in God's will. *The god who took away her legs. The god who took away my boy.*

Agnes led Clementine into the front room, where light cradled her, the smell of polished wood a balm. "You can have your old room back," Agnes said with a gentle pat on her hand like dry leaves falling with the promise of winter.

Clementine nodded and tried to smile. Then she walked with Earle to the back bedroom, where he touched her shoulder lightly before saying good night, as if he were afraid she might break. He looked at her with such kindness, she struggled to hold back tears.

"We'll see you in the morning, okay?"

Clementine nodded and entered the bedroom, leaving the door slightly ajar. Earle's heavy footsteps walked back down the hallway, and she heard him speak quietly to Agnes.

Their voices slowly lulled Clementine to sleep.

buried treasure

When Dorie awoke in her own room, sheets freshly laundered, house scrubbed clean, it felt strangely unfamiliar to her. After relinquishing her bed to Clementine for so many weeks, it was as if Clementine had imprinted herself there to remind Dorie of her absence. She still felt bruised after the awful scene the other night. All the progress they'd made, dissolved in an instant.

"At least you came back to me," she crooned to Rosie, stroking her ears. She had chosen her; they belonged to each other now. "Good girl. You came home, didn't you?"

Rosie rubbed against her legs and purred as an accompaniment to the gurgle and huff of the coffee maker. Dorie figured she could squeeze in a quick cup before Lynn picked her up. Her friend had called the day before to invite Dorie to Crabfest, an annual event every May that was visited by locals and tourists alike. Dorie's usual excuses had fallen on deaf ears.

"I won't take no for an answer. Clementine's gone. She's not your responsibility anymore."

"I know, you're right. I can't help worrying a little, though, wondering if she's okay, where she is."

"Shel told me she's staying at the ranch with the Beauchamps. Apparently, they knew each other. Anyway, they'll take good care of her."

Dorie had been surprised to feel relief that Clementine was safe, considering how angry she'd been just a few days before. Still, it was out of her hands now.

"You've done enough worrying to last a lifetime. You're coming out with me, and you're going to have some fun."

So Dorie had finally agreed to go and was determined to enjoy herself. She poured the coffee into a mug and went to the refrigerator for milk, pausing before she opened the door. Harriet's stick-figure family smiled back at her, tape rejoining their hands where a rip down the middle had torn them apart.

Lynn announced her arrival then by honking her horn several times outside the house. Dorie smiled. *She's right. I am glad to be rid of Clementine. Now I can focus on other things, like spending time with my new friends.*

"You ready for a good time?" Lynn asked as they pulled onto Highway 87. Her bright grin and messy topknot gave her a carefree air that Dorie hoped might rub off on her a little. "All righty, then. Let's get this show on the road!"

As they approached Crystal Beach, which was portioned off for the festivities, the sound of live music and the smell of fried food took Dorie back to her youth. Her family used to go to the Washington State Fair every year, and she and her brother would ditch their parents as soon as they could. They'd gorge themselves and get sick on rides that spun until their heads rattled.

Once, she'd gotten so ill, all she could do was sit with her head in her hands and groan. That was when her little brother had wandered off. She'd heard stories about carnies convincing youngsters to run away and join them for a life on the road, free spirits roaming from town to town. Dorie had been terrified he'd agreed to run away with them, and she spent what felt like hours searching for him.

She'd dreaded telling her parents, but when she finally gave up and went to confess, he'd been walking happily with them, eating another plate of fried dough sprinkled liberally with powdered sugar. Dorie remembered feeling relieved, disappointed, and angry that she'd spent all that wasted time worrying about him. But then he had handed her his still-full plate of funnel cake with that smile of his, and she'd loved him again.

Lynn parked the car, and they walked past a giant red octopus brimming with bouncing, screeching children. Lynn stopped at one booth. "Dorie, meet my friend Bea. She makes the best jam you've ever eaten, guaranteed!"

Bea had a round, pleasant face and wore a voluminous smock dress that made her look as if she'd stepped off a *Little House on the Prairie* set. She smiled at Dorie and extended a generous piece of bread topped with strawberry jam.

"What do you think?"

It tickled the back of Dorie's throat, the sticky sweetness forcing her lips to smack together so she could taste it again. "I'll take two jars."

"Maybe you can help us make some next time. Lynn usually gives me a hand," Bea said with a wide smile, seeming to enjoy Dorie's obvious pleasure.

Lynn and Bea chatted for a bit about what fruits Bea used and argued about the use of pectin versus a slow simmer. Dorie scanned the crowd of sunburned, cowboy-hatted, mostly scantily clad festivalgoers. Carl was back in town for the festival, playing on one of the smaller stages, so she wondered if she'd run into Rennie.

Then she spotted Kevin, the Tiki Man, a little apart from the crowds, on the edge of the entrance. She touched Lynn's arm to let her know where she was headed, pleased to see someone she recognized in this sea of strangers. As she moved closer to him, she could make out Willie Nelson's nasal tones coming from a radio, soothing to her ears among the more dissonant noises of the crowd.

Moving to the rhythms of the shore, the Tiki Man's sinewy body twisted and leaned with ease as he worked. A mermaid form awakened under his hands, under his blade, as he chiseled locks of seaweed, smoothed her curves. Dorie walked between the carved tikis that surrounded him, a rapt audience. She stroked the smoothness of their burnished surfaces.

He looked up when she reached him, his sawdust skin of creases and crevices marked by pilgrimages to find fallen trees that told him their secrets.

"I saw you on the beach a while back when you found a piece of driftwood—up by Rollover."

"Right," he said, continuing his work.

"Did it ever figure out what it wanted to be?"

"Nope, not yet. These things can take time."

She was disappointed not to witness the transformation. "I like your mermaid." She gestured, recalling Clementine with an unexpected surge of protectiveness that caught her off guard. It was almost physically painful, like a deep splinter.

Kevin put down his chisel. "She appeared from this old oak tree up on Broadway that had to come down. The owner was real attached to it and asked if I could salvage the wood and make something for him to remember it by."

"Well, I'm sure he'll be pleased."

"Hope so, hope so." He picked up a different tool and resumed his work. Chips of wood fell away from the mermaid's tail, littering the ground as he cut grooves into scales. The scent of resin and salt fused with an image of Clementine wandering along the water.

As Dorie made her way back to find Lynn, she passed a group of giggling girls. One of them half galloped, half danced ahead, her body's edges and angles moving loosely, like a puppet on strings. Izzie followed behind, handing a bottle to another girl. Her friend drank from it and winced as she swallowed. Then Izzie caught up to the dancing girl and shared the bottle with her, their laughter growing louder.

A group of boys nearby looked over at them, their eyes bleary with beer and teenage lust. One of them shouted, "Hey, Iz. Get your fine ass over here, girl!"

The trouble Rennie had mentioned obviously wasn't just academic, then.

Lynn arrived next to Dorie and pulled her along. "Come on! We have to find the crab shack. I'm starving!"

Dorie decided not to mention seeing Izzie; she didn't want to cause trouble. Notes from a fiddle danced through the crowd, tripping playfully between people's feet. Dorie's senses were in overload as a small, sticky child raced by them, clutching a fish-shaped balloon and screaming for her friend to wait up.

"Over there!" Lynn cried.

They sped toward a line several yards long. The wait was worth every minute. After filling their plates, they found a shady table and barely spoke a word as they ate, until all that remained were empty red shards sucked clean.

"Make sure you save room for gumbo. There's a cook off." Lynn wiped her buttery face with a napkin. "We have to find Pete; you've got to meet him. He's the one who caught most of these suckers."

Pete—the guy who Lou was working for. Dorie wondered if Lou would be here as well.

"He's a descendant of Jean Lafitte, you know."

"Who?" Dorie held her full stomach, doubtful she'd be able to partake of the gumbo.

"Pete."

"No, who's Jean La . . . ?"

"He was a pirate who settled in Galveston for a while, but he partied here on Bolivar. More remote, less likely to get into trouble. Not so different from today, actually. I think a large number of us locals are descendants of pirates." Lynn suddenly developed a pirate's brogue. "And *mighty proud of it!*"

Lynn finished the last of her beer. "Easier for smugglers over here too. Safer place to bury all that treasure."

"Has any ever been found?"

"A couple of silver bars were dug up once."

Dorie wondered what other buried treasure might be hidden there and imagined uncovering a ruby-encrusted sword hilt stolen from a king, an Indian arrowhead stained with enemy blood, or a handwritten love letter sealed in a glass bottle banded with gold. Or perhaps even a broken heart buried deep, deep down that needed to be dug up, brought back into the light, and mended by healing hands.

"My friend Shirley flies a skull and crossbones whenever she's on her period."

Dorie laughed as she had long ago, during those endless summer days of childhood when all she did was sleep late, swim, and read. She felt a lightness that she'd forgotten existed. "So is Pete a pirate, like his great . . . whatever?"

"Well, he doesn't *pillage*, as far as I know, but you can't keep him off the water, and he does enjoy a good time. He looks kind of like a pirate too, especially now that he's older. Crazy long hair, full beard, wicked eyes."

Dorie imagined *Treasure Island*'s Long John Silver with a Texas accent and laughed again.

"Goddamn!" continued Lynn. "I had such a crush on him when I was younger! Bad, he was. Bad like a pirate!" Lynn's eyes widened and then glazed over with a faraway look. "We fooled around a few times. I remember the first time. We were at a party up near High Island. My parents hated me going there at night; no one up to any good went to High Island after dark. So I was already kind of nervous. I swear, he swaggered—always had a cigarette hanging out the side of his mouth. He rode a motorcycle, of course—my mama wouldn't ever let me ride on one, so we had to sneak."

The image in Dorie's head morphed into a young Marlon Brando as she continued listening to Lynn's story.

"My friend Debbie's older sister drove us girls to the party. We tried to sip whiskey around the fire, and I acted as if I hadn't noticed him. When he drank, he'd get bawdy and sing at the top of his lungs, his gold earring catching the firelight, hypnotizing all the girls into loving him."

Lynn focused her gaze back on Dorie and slapped the table lightly. "But I grew out of bad boys eventually. In fact, Ken is one of the sweetest guys I know. Besides Rennie, of course."

Dorie shifted in her seat. "Will we catch Carl playing while we're here?"

"Of course! Wouldn't miss it for the world." Lynn stood up. "We better get some more partying in before he's on. Let's go!"

Dorie rose and shook her skirt free of tiny slivers of crab shell and bread crumbs. "So where to next?"

"Onward, me hearty!" Lynn yelled in her pirate brogue as they reentered the fray.

A crowd had already started to form close to the stage, sweaty, sunburned bodies moving to canned music blasting from the speakers. They were sucked into the melee as by the pull of an undertow, helpless to fight it. The anticipation of the crowd waiting to see a local boy about to hit the big time was palpable.

Dorie was a bit hazy from too much sun and all the food and beer she'd consumed over the last few hours. She could either give into it and enjoy the evening or admit defeat and go home to sleep it all off.

She spied Carl not far ahead, shaking hands with a skinny man who looked up at him with pride. He looked familiar. Then Dorie saw his date and remember the drunk couple from Coconuts. They soon began shimmying to the music, Walt stumbling every once in a while. Carl moved on, getting pats on the back and handshakes, until he reached Rennie, who was talking to a striking woman. She smiled and put her hand on Carl's arm. He leaned closer to hear her over the racket and then gave her a hug and walked toward the stage.

"Who's that?" asked Dorie, pointing and trying her best to sound nonchalant.

"Oh, no."

"What?"

"That's Claire. She's such a bitch."

That was Claire? Dorie felt a jolt in her stomach. She started to ask Lynn about her, but at that moment, the lights dimmed, and a pre-climactic hush fell over the crowd as they waited for Carl's entrance. He sauntered onto the stage from the wings, hugging his guitar and grinning his lopsided grin as the crowd roared.

"Howdy! Thanks for comin' out tonight. Good to see

familiar faces and a few new ones too. I can't tell y'all how happy I am to be back in the old stompin' grounds. As many of you folks know, I'm an adopted local—y'all helped raise me, right?"

The crowd went berserk—hollering and stamping their feet in unison.

"So this song's a new one I just wrote. Sure hope you like it."

The sound of Carl's guitar broke through the screams as he opened with a catchy tune. He tapped into a pulse that resonated with people on a level that made local boys into stars. His Texas drawl elongated the lyrics into an aching whine that flattened and rose, scratching and then falling lazily into a low mumble, quieting the audience, reminding them of broken hearts, whiskey nights, and rambling days.

Dorie spent the next half hour watching Carl perform out of one eye and trying *not* to watch Rennie and Claire out of the other. She'd never seen this version of Rennie before. He seemed tense, and she couldn't help wondering whether it was because he didn't want to be next to Claire or because he did.

Carl made his last encore, and the crowd finally began to realize that no matter how much they kept cheering for him, the show was over. Dorie wanted to tell Rennie how impressed she was, to share in his joy and pride. But she couldn't see him anymore and assumed he'd gone to find Carl.

"Come on. Time to go." Lynn led her through a gap in the crowd. "Let's try to beat the masses to the parking lot, or we'll be here all night."

"Shouldn't we find Carl and congratulate him?"

"We'd never find him in this mess. We can congratulate him at the party tomorrow."

"The party?"

"Didn't Rennie call you?" Dorie was embarrassed for Lynn, who had obviously assumed she was invited.

"No, he didn't."

"Oh. Weird. Well, I'm sure he will. He must be busy with all the preparations and stuff. He probably assumed Shel had already invited you."

Dorie imagined the "and stuff" part probably involved Claire. They passed through throngs of parents carrying sleepy kids, partyers slopping warm beer from plastic cups, restroom lines snaking through the crowd. Dorie wondered where Rennie and Claire were headed and hoped Claire would live up to her "bitch" status and not charm her way back into Rennie's life.

what it is we need

Clementine woke again to the perpetual feeling of displacement, softened only by the aroma of the fresh biscuits Agnes must have made while she slept. Every day since Clementine had arrived, Agnes had prepared breakfast. At first, she hadn't been able to eat, but after a few days, Clementine's stomach had responded to the delicious aromas that greeted her each morning.

Today, the bright kitchen beckoned, and she lifted a clean linen towel off the plate of still-warm biscuits, golden with melted butter. Salt coaxed her taste buds back to life, and she took a second biscuit as she made her way to the living room.

"You're up." Agnes sat in her chair by the window, her fingers moving over the rosary beads she held in her lap. Earle sat close by, reading the paper. "There are biscuits in the kitchen, if you're hungry." Clementine wiped her mouth of any stray crumbs, and Agnes smiled. "I see you found them. Good. Now come sit with us for a bit." Agnes gestured to the velvet sofa beside her.

An oversized photograph of Agnes standing next to a large chestnut horse hung on the wall next to them. She was holding the reins loosely, and the horse's head was bowed, seeming to caress her cheek with its own. Clementine could almost hear its cavernous breath, smell the musky scent of beast and land. She'd often wanted to ask Agnes about it, and now she could, as if her own loss gave her permission to share in Agnes's.

"When was that taken?"

Agnes followed her gaze to the photograph. "Oh, a long time ago now. Shortly before I lost Levi. And had my accident." Earle looked up at the photo and then over at Agnes.

"What happened?" asked Clementine.

"Levi got out of the pasture and ran into the highway. I raced after him, tried to get him off the road. But he was too spooked and wouldn't come." Earle winced and closed his eyes, as if trying to erase the memory. "When I finally reached him, we were hit by a truck. Levi had to be put down, and I ended up in this chair."

Earle moved closer to Agnes. "She rode for hours, every day, ever since I first met her." He looked at Agnes. "First time I saw her ride, I knew I'd spend the rest of my days loving her. And if she loved me back, I'd make sure I deserved her."

Clementine had never heard Earle speak that way before. Whenever she cleaned their house, they had treated her with decency and some care. But she had been their employee first and foremost. When they brought her to stay with them after she lost Finn, she hadn't been able to speak or listen. She'd existed in a liminal space that felt like a refuge of sorts, one she'd needed more than a warm bed and concerned looks.

Now, she sensed they'd all crossed over a line that permitted a level of intimacy without bounds.

Agnes chuckled. "Don't you have work to do, Earle?" He stood and kissed her hand before leaving the room, his shoulders a little straighter as Agnes watched him walk away, still smiling. Then she turned to Clementine. "So tell me, where have you been this whole time?"

Clementine hardly knew where to start. "I've been staying with a . . ." *What is Dorie? No longer my Keeper. A friend?* "Her name's Dorie."

Agnes's expression shifted for a moment, and Clementine wondered if perhaps she had expected her to return to them sooner, their home a place of sanctuary that she would instinctively have been drawn back to. And she had been. It had just taken a little time for her to find her place.

"Why did you leave her?"

"She took my house from me. My life."

"It's her house now, Clementine."

Clementine stiffened. "All my things are gone. There's nothing left."

"Dorie means well, I think." Agnes paused. "She came here looking for you a while back."

Clementine tried not to remember the look on Dorie's face when she'd walked in the door after the lighthouse dinner. "I didn't ask her to take care of me."

"We don't always ask for what it is we need."

"But she read my journal. I thought she was trying to help me, that she understood me because of our shared . . . because of Finn and Harriet."

Her voice caught as she said the names aloud, as if the months without Finn had rendered the sound of his name obsolete, leaving it to exist only in her past life, not this one.

"That journal was private."

"Perhaps it needed to be found."

Clementine imagined Dorie finding it hidden away in a

cupboard somewhere, discarded and forgotten. Her fingers leaving their imprints in the leather cover as Clementine's own had, the words mingling with Dorie's own memories. *Which I destroyed.* Bile rose in her throat as she saw Dorie staring at Harriet's torn picture, their shared sorrow becoming one.

everybody smile wide

*d*orie hurried up and down the aisles of The Big Store, trying to ignore the screaming children and half-clothed, sunburned shoppers, wanting to escape the mayhem as soon as possible. It was always busy during the peak summer season, when tourists took over the peninsula. Out-of-towners would overbuy for their vacations, when diets and restraint went out the window: hot dogs and sides of beef for grilling, cases of beer and margarita mix, huge tubs of ice cream.

As Dorie turned the corner of the produce aisle, she almost collided with a shopping cart being pushed much too quickly by a young boy. He stopped just short of hitting her. His mother hurried over, grabbing him impatiently.

"Johnny, be careful—Oh! Hi, Dorie!"

It was Shelley, who looked as harried as the first time Dorie had met her at Coconuts. Perhaps even more so. Her cut-off jean shorts dangled loose threads, and her bare feet were on full display, her chipped pedicure even pinker than the sequined flip-flops she wore.

"I'm so sorry about Johnny. He's in a hurry to get home."

Izzie walked languidly toward them, her arms filled with chip bags. She was almost unrecognizable from Crabfest the day before. Her face was bare of makeup, and she wore her hair in pigtails that should have made her look younger but oddly had the opposite effect.

"Hello, Izzie," said Dorie. Izzie just looked at her.

"Say hello to Mrs. Edwards, Izzie," ordered her mom.

"Hi," Izzie said in a sullen monotone. Dorie noticed a look pass between mother and daughter, and Izzie stood taller, straightening her shoulders.

"I hope you're coming to the party tonight," Shelley said excitedly. Dorie cleared her throat, not sure how to respond. "Please come. We want to show Carl how much we love him, and it'll be a great place for you to meet more neighbors. Lynn will be there. And Rennie, of course." Dorie assumed the striking but bitchy Claire would be there too. She wondered if that was why Rennie hadn't invited her himself. "We'll see you at my place around six."

Shelley took the shopping cart from Johnny and started back down the aisle. "Watch your brother, Izzie!" Izzie dumped the chip bags into the cart and grabbed her little brother's shirt, half dragging the now-screaming boy down the aisle, sliding her feet as if she couldn't be bothered to lift them.

As Dorie passed the wine and beer aisle at the back of the store, she picked up a bottle of champagne. It was a celebration for Carl, after all. Or perhaps beer would be better; Rennie preferred beer. Dorie wasn't sure she could handle another big event so soon, but she should show her support for Carl—and Rennie, the proud dad.

Shelley's pink house was decorated with streamers and an absurd number of balloons tied to the deck railings, so that Dorie imagined it might float up high over the ocean and disappear with everyone still in it.

Now that would be a party worth going to.

Music blared from multiple speakers placed strategically around the front yard, which was bordered by oversized pink hibiscus, like cartoon flowers. On the concrete deck below, smoke billowed from three barbecue pits, filling the air with the aroma of grilled meat.

"Dorie! Over here!" Lynn waved at her. She looped arms with the man standing next to her. "This is Pete. Pete, my friend Dorie."

Lou's employer and Lynn's high school crush. He did resemble a pirate—lean and scraggly, his multiple tattoos lost in crepe-paper creases of loose skin. Pete held up a beer in greeting, his eyes already slightly bleary.

"Have a daiquiri. They're yummy!" Lynn sucked on her fluorescent-red drink.

"I think I'll wait a bit, thanks. I'm still recovering from last night."

"Ain't you never heard of hair o' the dog?" Pete winked at her as he turned toward the bar nearby and poured her a drink from a large pitcher.

"Oh. Well, thanks." It was too red and too sweet, but she drank some down anyway.

"Let's go see Carl," said Lynn, disengaging from Pete and pulling Dorie toward the other side of the deck. Dorie followed her as she pushed her way through the circle of girls surrounding Carl. "You were amazing last night! We're so proud of you!" She gave him a long hug, the girls obviously wishing they were in Lynn's place. "How's the tour going?"

"Pretty good. It sure is good to be back for a while, though."

Dorie supposed the peninsula anchored him after being shuttled back and forth throughout his childhood. He looked tired, as if he'd rather be at home in bed than at a party thrown in his honor. She remembered his shine on stage the previous night and noticed the contrast in the boy standing before her now.

"Honey! Come on over here! I wanna take your picture!"

"Be right there, Mom. Excuse me" Carl slowly made his way over to Claire, who had collected a group of people, readying to pose. Her eyes lingered slightly on Dorie as she waited for Carl to navigate through the pats on the back and noises of congratulations that impeded his path.

Claire was dressed unlike anyone else at the party. No shorts, tee shirt, or flip-flops for her. She wore a green silk dress and heels, her dark-red hair falling in perfect waves around her heavily made-up face. Dorie regretted not making more of an effort for the party. She hadn't bothered with makeup because she'd known she would just sweat it off anyway, although she had managed a bit of lipstick. Dorie couldn't decide if Claire was beautiful or simply well put together.

Claire handed the camera over and stood in the center, her arms around Carl and Rennie, four other guests arranged behind them. "Everybody smile wide," she said before flashing incongruously imperfect teeth in a picture-posing smile. It was, Dorie decided, Claire's imperfect teeth, a bit crooked and very slightly yellow, that made her truly beautiful. Dorie tucked a frizz of hair behind her ear, wondering how many imperfections Claire saw in her. Much too many for her to be considered beautiful, she was sure.

Lynn continued introducing her to countless people,

until she was overwhelmed and exhausted. She drank her daiquiri faster than she had planned, probably from nerves, and someone nearby good-naturedly replaced her empty glass with another.

Shelley suddenly appeared. "Dorie, you came!" She pulled her into a hug and then stepped back, grabbing her daughter's arm as she passed. "Say hello, Iz."

This time, Izzie's pale skin contrasted with almost-black lipstick, eyes outlined heavily in dark kohl, all covered with a veil of long jet-black hair. The effect was her face receding into darkness. Dorie wondered if she'd gotten into trouble last night for drinking, if she'd been drinking today as well, and she consciously tried not to stare at her.

"Hi, Izzie. Are you enjoying the party?" Dorie asked.

Shelley nudged her. "Yes, ma'am."

"You must be very proud of your cousin."

Izzie looked over at Carl, who was now talking to Rennie and Claire. "Yes, ma'am."

Carl and his parents made their way over then. "You must introduce me, Rennie," Claire said, looking too closely at Dorie with a pinched smile.

Rennie avoided eye contact with them both. "Claire, this is Dorie."

Claire held out a well-manicured hand. "Hello. I hope everyone has given you a warm welcome." Dorie reluctantly took her hand, Claire's cool palm meeting Dorie's, which was clammy from the ninety-plus-degree heat and humidity. Claire removed her hand and placed it on Rennie's shoulder. "So, how do you like living here on the peninsula? I hear you moved from Houston—quite a change, I expect."

"It is." She wondered if Rennie had talked about her much to Claire, and if so, what exactly he'd said. "But I prefer a quieter life these days." Dorie watched Claire's hand squeeze

Rennie's shoulder. "Though I'm starting to realize it's not always so quiet around here." She attempted a laugh that came out flat and distorted.

"Yeah, we sure do know how to have a good time." Claire looked up at Rennie and flipped her hair over her shoulder. "Still, it's not the same as city life, is it? I imagine, after what all you've been through, it must be tempting to be in a more secluded spot—away from it all."

So Rennie *had* talked about her. "I suppose so," she stuttered, not trusting the direction Claire was taking the conversation.

Rennie cleared his throat. "Claire doesn't appreciate it here; she prefers the city."

"I do. I live in New Orleans—best city in the world!" She flipped her hair again, and it fell perfectly back into place. "I miss Carl terribly, of course. It's so hard to watch them grow up and not need their mamas anymore."

Dorie realized she was gritting her teeth. Claire paused for a second and looked at Dorie, who tried to nod, her mouth dry so that she couldn't swallow.

"But he's independent now and traveling the country, making a name for himself. My baby's becoming a star!" Claire beamed her imperfect smile.

Dorie's heart beat harder. "You're a very fortunate woman."

"I am." Claire reached out and ruffled Carl's hair. He jerked his head away quickly, smoothing his hair back into place.

Dorie felt heat rush through her. "I hope you realize how lucky you are to have watched your son grow up."

Claire looked at Rennie, her eyebrows raised, lips pursed as if questioning Dorie's sanity. When she spoke again, her voice was sickly sweet, and her words seemed to stick to Dorie's skin. "I didn't mean to imply—"

"How lucky you are that he doesn't need you anymore," Dorie added, her voice rising. "That he can leave here and live his life!" Her voice caught, and she breathed hard.

"Well, really." Claire looked from Dorie back to Rennie. "I didn't mean anything by it."

"I'm sure." Dorie tried to catch her breath, unable to say more.

Claire's composure wavered, her eyes hardening. Then she turned to Rennie. "Come on, darling."

Wobbling slightly in her high heels as she walked away, she reached her hand back for Rennie. When she realized he hadn't followed her, she stopped and looked back. Rennie glanced up at Dorie and then over to Claire, shaking his head slowly. Then he walked away in the opposite direction.

"Well, that was fun," said Lynn. Dorie closed her eyes, wishing herself gone. "No one ever calls her out. Not even Rennie."

"Yes, I noticed." Why had Rennie let Claire talk to her like that? He shouldn't have been discussing her with Claire anyway.

"I should have done it myself years ago. Way to go, Dorie!" She put her arm around Dorie's shoulders and squeezed. "From now on, no more faking. I'll treat Claire the same way she's always treated me."

"And how is that?"

"Come on over here." Lynn guided Dorie through the crowd to a quieter spot behind the house. "So we can talk."

They sat down on a stark wooden bench next to a fish-cleaning station, the smell of which made Dorie slightly nauseous. "God, how could he stand being with someone like that?" Dorie asked.

Lynn shook her head. "You know, I never did figure out what Rennie ever saw in her. She's exotic, I suppose—glamorous, ambitious. I guess Rennie was attracted to that in the beginning. He loved her, but I don't know that he actually *liked* her much." That part, Dorie found easy to imagine. "Anyway, she's just jealous."

"Jealous?"

"Of Rennie and you."

"Don't be ridiculous. There's no Rennie and me."

"If you say so," said Lynn.

"Anyway, I can't imagine what he thinks of me now. And Carl—oh god."

"Don't worry. Rennie is well aware of his ex-wife's mean streak, believe me. Hell, he's probably as impressed with you as I am. I didn't know you had it in you."

Dorie hadn't either. "Were you guys friends?"

"Well, I tried to like her for Rennie's sake, but it was a challenge, I can tell you. When she was pregnant with Carl, she'd go on and on to me about how wonderful it was to carry a child and bring it into this world. But Rennie told me all she did around him was bitch about how fat and tired she always felt. Me and Ken had been trying to have a baby for years by that point. Until we figured out that we can't have children."

So many childless mothers: Lynn, Clementine, me. None of us will ever get to experience the joy of watching our children grow and leave to start their own lives full of exploration, failure, discovery, fulfillment, and love. Only Claire has that privilege.

The insistent odor of scorched meat permeated Dorie's pores, her body limp and numb. She suddenly felt very tired.

"Lynn, I think it's time for me to call it a night. I'm going to go."

"Are you crazy? The party hasn't even started yet." Lynn stood up and began shaking her hips to the music, as if trying to replace the moment of melancholy with an urgent need to move her body. "Carl's best friend is deejaying, and we've got some serious dancing to do!" She threw back her head, her long blonde hair flying free from its clip.

That was the last thing Dorie wanted to do. "I'm sorry, but it's been a long day."

"Okay, party pooper! Your loss." Lynn scanned the crowd forming close to the speakers for a more willing partner, and Dorie made a quick exit before anyone else tried to convince her to stay.

close to her heart

*H*umidity hung thick in the still air. Even though Clementine sat on the tire swing under the shade of the oak tree, her blouse stuck to her back and strands of damp hair coiled around her face. She opened her eyes as footsteps approached.

Earle took off his hat and wiped his forehead with his sleeve. "Today's a real scorcher."

He stood beside her for a bit, looking into the distance. "Look here. I have something for you." He dug into his pocket and pulled out a thin silver chain. "I gave this to Agnes a long time ago." He draped it carefully over his fingers so it caught the sunlight filtering through the branches. "We want you to have it now." He held it out to her. "For Finn's shell."

Clementine reached up to where the shell sat in the hollow of her throat. "But it's too special to give away."

"That's why we want you to have it."

Clementine paused, then tugged at the worn string around her throat, snapping it a final time. She placed it in her pocket and handed the shell to Earle, who carefully strung it onto the chain.

"Allow me." He walked behind her. She lifted her hair for Earle to place the chain around her neck and waited patiently as he fumbled with the fastener.

"There you go," he said, stepping in front of her again.

The shell had settled into place, close to Clementine's heart.

palimpsest

*d*orie had been waiting at Shelley's door for several minutes. *Where on earth is Izzie?*

She felt a tinge of guilt at her annoyance. Shelley had undoubtedly felt the same way when Dorie had missed some sessions after she first took Clementine in. Dorie hoped she hadn't contributed to Izzie failing her English class last semester. Izzie was now in summer school and needed to pass. Dorie would make damn sure that happened this time.

She went down the wooden stairs and checked under the house, where an old pickup with mottled paint sagged in the summer heat. Then she made her way down the road toward the beach. That was when she saw her, sitting with someone, tucked between two dunes. Dorie watched as they leaned toward each other and started making out heavily. As a teacher, she'd broken up many a tryst, and that instinct kicked in.

"Izzie." They disengaged at the sound of her voice. "Did you forget our appointment today?"

Izzie smoothed back her disheveled black hair, obviously

flustered. As she did, Dorie took a closer look at Izzie's make-out partner. The cropped-short haircut had misled her for a minute, but it was obvious now that she was a girl about the same age as Izzie. They both stood up.

"I'll see you later, Kel," Izzie said as her friend walked away, her loose limbs too long for her body—the girl from Crabfest. Dorie drew her attention back to Izzie, who looked at her now with fierce defiance. "You can't tell my mom or Rennie about this."

Dorie was at a loss for words.

"Really. You can't. They wouldn't understand."

"Okay. But are you sure? They care about you and want what's best for you."

"No. They want what's easiest for my mom to deal with. And believe me, this is not something she'd be able to deal with."

"What about Rennie? He seems like he'd understand."

"No. Anyway, he'd just tell my mom. He acts like he's my dad or something."

Dorie wondered then about Izzie's father. No one had mentioned him at all.

"He worries about you."

"Yeah, I know he does. Everyone worries about me, *all* the time."

Dorie sighed. "Look, none of this alters the fact that you're late for our session. Let's go." Dorie walked back to the house, Izzie trailing behind.

When they sat down at the table, Dorie was eager to discuss the book Izzie was reading for school and avoid any further discussion of her personal life. It would be difficult to keep something so important from Rennie, and she was annoyed that Izzie had put her in such a difficult position.

"In *To Kill a Mockingbird*, Atticus Finch argues that Tom

Robinson didn't rape Mayella but that she was repeatedly abused by her father. Yet Tom is still sentenced by the jury. What are your thoughts on this injustice?"

"That society is backward and racist. People judge others for stupid reasons. It's not fair."

"That's true. It isn't fair. Scout and her brother learn a difficult lesson about human nature."

"At least I can hide, unlike Tom."

"You can't hide forever."

"I won't. I'm leaving this place as soon as I graduate. One more year, and I'm outta here."

"Well, meanwhile, if you need someone to talk to, I'm here."

Izzie looked up from the book and into Dorie's eyes, her face shifting from defiance to a vulnerability that Dorie hadn't seen before—a palimpsest with layers that obscured the original image beneath.

They became so engrossed in their session that Dorie was surprised when she heard voices outside the front door. Izzie's brothers rushed into the room and started digging through the first grocery bag Shelley dumped on the kitchen counter.

"Still at it?" Shelley asked as she started unpacking the bags.

"We went a bit over today. Had a very productive discussion, didn't we, Izzie?"

Izzie looked at Dorie and nodded.

"She's coming along very well. With her understanding of the book."

Shelley put a gallon of orange soda in the fridge. "Great. Keep it up, Iz." She didn't catch her daughter's barely contained grimace as Izzie got up to help her mother unpack. "I have to head to work in a bit. Watch your brothers, Iz. I'll be home late."

Dorie lingered for a moment, hoping Shelley wouldn't forget her check again, though it was usually Rennie who ended up paying for the tutoring sessions. Everyone seemed caught up in their own duties, though, so she said her good-byes and left.

Dorie hoped Izzie would tell Shelley or Rennie about herself sooner rather than later. She knew from teaching in the city, where people tended to be a bit more open-minded about these things, that it was important not to interfere between kids and their families when it came to such matters.

One student at her school had attempted to take his own life because he was afraid to tell his parents, thought they'd reject him when they found out he was gay. Afterward, when he told them, they all became heavily involved in supporting the LBGTQ community.

Izzie's secret needed to be told. Dorie just wasn't sure whether it was she who should tell it.

nourishment

*C*lementine dozed in and out of dreams, the smell of her childhood rubbing against her like a cat wanting affection. Maria, she of gentle lisps and lilts, sang songs of longing and sadness as she worked. Songs for Clementine's father, who had lost his only love. And for his daughter, who paid the price.

Maria stirred the huge pot of menudo, Clementine's favorite—nourishment for her body and soul—reminding Clementine that she learned to love from her *niñera*. That she can love. The pot bubbled and plopped on the iron stove, an accompaniment to Maria's lament.

Clementine stood as close as Maria would let her when she was cooking, holding her *niñera's* blue cotton skirt with sticky fingers. She smelled the remnants of cumin that had brushed against the hem when Maria gathered it from the herb garden earlier that morning. It mingled with the chiles that would make Clementine's lips tingle as she slurped the soup from her bowl, the spices and herbs penetrating her taste buds so she would smell it hours later.

When Clementine opened her eyes to the sunlight entering the window, the taste from her dream lingered still, and she could almost feel the spongy tripe dissolving in her mouth. She got out of bed, forgetting for a moment that she was at Agnes's rather than in her childhood bedroom, with terrace doors wide open to the orchard and mountains beyond.

"I have a surprise for you," said Agnes when Clementine entered the kitchen. But Clementine knew what it was before she saw it on the stove. "Sit. Eat." Agnes put a bowl in front of her, and she inhaled the scent of Maria's love. The taste from her dream now made real.

"How did you know?" Clementine asked, lifting a spoonful to her lips, which were already tingling in anticipation.

"It wasn't me. A gift. He brought it this morning while you were sleeping."

"Who?"

"Lou. Said it's your favorite. Told me he hopes he got it right." Clementine ate another mouthful and then another. "I guess he got it right," said Agnes, smiling and patting the table.

After eating, Clementine went out into the yard to feed the chickens for Agnes. They squawked and flapped in a frenzy of white feathers, perhaps wondering why Finn wasn't helping. Silly, to think that they would remember her boy, feel his absence as she did. But it was inconceivable that the space he left in this world could not be felt acutely by every other living thing.

Her ears picked up voices coming from the barn, both so familiar to her. She couldn't make out their words, but the cadence and intonation reminded her of poems she'd had to memorize in school—a part of her subconscious that resurfaced without will or intent. Outside the barn doors were carcasses of giant beasts, oxidized blood-red ribs of rusted metal, sharp-toothed jaws once able to snap bones in half like twigs. As she drew closer, the beasts revealed their true selves, and the sounds separated.

"Help me lift this thresher, will ya? This old back don't work as well as it used to."

Grunts and puffs of exertion were emitted from the dusty barn, as if from the beast's lair. But emerging from the shadows were Earle and Lou, carrying an old farm implement of some sort.

"Just set it there. I'll have Ennis come pick up all the junk tomorrow. Once we got everything cleared outta here, it shouldn't take too much to build this out. Just patch it up some, add ventilation—"

That's when they saw her.

"Mornin', Clementine. You're up early." Earle glanced over at Lou, who ran his hand through his dusty hair. "Lou here is helping me around the ranch a bit. My back's been giving me some trouble."

Earle rubbed his lower spine to illustrate his point, and Clementine noticed his slight stoop next to Lou's straight, strong body. His words got lost as she watched Lou wipe the sweat from his face with his shirt, leaving smudges of grime that she had to stop herself from rubbing away.

"Hi, Clem. How are you?" Lou said it quietly, as if hoping not to frighten her away.

"I'm okay . . ."

Lou smiled. Not the roguish grin she knew from when they'd first met, but a smile that was a map of his journey from then to now.

"Let's go, Lou. We got lots more work to do here."

When she looked at Earle, he was watching her with what she imagined were a father's eyes. They reentered the faded red barn, and she sat on the dusty ground, watching them work, surrounded by the white chickens.

Soon, another man exited the barn carrying paint cans, which he set down beside scaffolding that climbed the walls like vines.

"You start on this wall, Rennie. Lou, go on over there. We'll each take a side, and we should be done by dinnertime. Lou's got soup on the stove just waitin' to be et." Earle directed them with the assurance of a man accustomed to running a crew, and all three started painting the exterior of the barn bright red. Their strokes were long and slow, the rhythm of waves lapping.

Clementine moved closer and smelled cluttered studios, canvases stacked against walls, brushes shoved into plastic cartons, Pollock paint splatters covering every surface. She reached for a brush resting on top of an open can and pushed it through the paint skin, which resisted slightly, its creamy density tempting her. When she lifted the brush, it dripped red drops onto the ground. A blood sacrifice. She stroked the wooden siding, turning it bright, lost in the familiar rhythm: up, down, dip, up, down, dip . . .

When she finally stopped, she found Lou watching as if he were seeing her for the first time.

stingaree

Walking up the wooden stairs of Stingaree, Dorie inhaled the smells of the marina. She stopped to pet one of the stray cats that wandered around begging for scraps of food and love, like Rosie had probably done before they found each other. She'd have to remember to save some scraps from lunch as a special treat for Rosie.

Perhaps I'll order crab, her favorite. Although she's getting quite fat and spoiled. Like me.

Then she reached the top step, and a wave of anxiety rippled through her. She hadn't seen Rennie since Carl's party and had been surprised when he invited her to lunch. She wasn't at all sure what to expect. She couldn't help resenting him for not sticking up for her at the party, but she also missed him and wanted to see him again.

Rennie was waiting at the bar when she walked in, and she noticed he looked particularly clean-shaven and neatly dressed. He greeted her, touching her shoulder, and she resisted the urge to lean into him as if she were one of the cats downstairs. They walked to a table by the window over-looking the bay and ordered iced tea and the special.

"So how are things?" asked Rennie.

"It's nice to be out; I've had a bit of cabin fever, I think." Rennie smiled, and Dorie looked out the window at the water, searching for something else to say. "Is Carl back out on the road already?"

"Yep. Have to get used to him being gone all over again." Rennie fiddled with a packet of sugar and cleared his throat. "Hey, I'm sorry about the party."

Dorie looked up at him, charmed by his unexpected awkwardness.

Rennie shifted in his seat. "I guess I worried you'd think less of me for having been with someone like that. She's no good for me. I see that even more clearly now. Wish I'd realized it before I married her."

Dorie's stomach fluttered. "We all make mistakes, misjudge people."

"I'm just glad Carl isn't like her. Doesn't have a mean bone in his body."

Dorie smiled. "I hear he gets his singing talent from her."

"I'll give her that."

Stingaree was crowded and noisy, and as Dorie looked around, she saw families laughing and couples whispering close. She wondered if they'd ever accept her as their own or if she still stuck out like a sore thumb, an outsider.

"I'm pleased to see Iz getting something out of your tutoring sessions," said Rennie. "She did pretty well on her last paper." Dorie wondered if he knew what else they'd shared besides literature. "She's a funny kid. One minute, she can't stand us and is practically failing out of school, and the next, she can't stop ranting about injustice and freedom. She's smart, but too easily misguided."

"Perhaps not misguided, just confused. Trying to figure out her place in the world."

"Well, she doesn't always make the best choices, if you ask me. Gets herself into too much trouble, skipping class and sneaking out with boys."

So she hadn't told them. Dorie squirmed in her chair, conflicted about sharing with Rennie what she knew. She hated that they had this secret between them.

"We've been reading *To Kill a Mockingbird* together," continued Rennie. "It's funny. I remember being assigned that book in high school, but I don't believe I ever read it, at least not properly."

"And how do you like it?" She tried to imagine Rennie and Izzie sitting together on the couch, taking turns reading passages from the book. She wanted to be there too.

"Well, Atticus Finch—he reminds me of my grandfather—a good man."

She realized then that Rennie had qualities similar to that character's, so lovingly written—patience, kindness, a quiet appreciation for the world he lived in and the people in it. Like Atticus, he had a way of understanding people, of walking in their shoes. She was sure he'd support Izzie if he knew the truth about her. But Izzie trusted Dorie not to say anything. Dorie's sense of loyalty to both Rennie and his niece weighed heavily. But Izzie needed someone to talk to who wouldn't judge, who could be on her side.

"Is Lou still staying with Pete?"

"He is. Did you know he's been helping Earle out a bit at the ranch?"

Dorie was surprised by the news. "Really? I didn't think they knew each other."

"I think he's doing it mostly to impress Clementine. To be near her, I guess."

"How does Clementine feel about him being there?"

"She seems okay, I think. We're clearing out the barn for her. Lou's idea. He thought she might start painting again, use it as her studio." Dorie wasn't sure how well that would go down after her own rejected attempts to get Clementine to paint. "It helps that Lou's stopped drinking, much to Pete's disappointment. I mean, most everyone I know probably drinks more than they should, but with Lou, it's different. He gets himself into trouble. I told Pete the other day, he reminds me of Bob's tiger."

"Tiger?"

"Bob collects exotic animals—he's really good with them. I'll take you over there sometime, if you like." She imagined a tiger roaming around Bob's bar, being petted by the customers like the stray cats under the restaurant. "He's lost all his fight now—more a pet than a wild animal."

"Who, the tiger or Lou?"

Rennie smiled. "Both, I suppose."

She took a sip of tea, her stomach growling as she watched their waitress carry a platter laden with steaming crab and corn on the cob to the next table. "I just don't know how I feel about Lou and Clementine as a couple. I'm not sure they're good for each other."

Rennie laughed dryly. "Isn't that for them to decide? Anyway, choosing who to love can be a tricky business."

"Do we even choose? I think it just happens."

"True enough."

Their waitress arrived and set down their order. The clatter of dishes and silverware, the waitress's chatter, and the steaming platter of crab claws eased them both back to the matter at hand. Rennie tore into the crab, and Dorie watched him eat for a minute, ready to relish all the good things in life as much as he did.

sin and forgiveness

*A*gnes and Earle came through the front door into the living room, dressed for church. Agnes wore a purple dress and matching hat that complemented her silver hair and dark skin. Earle had on a brown suit and formal cowboy hat that he removed as he sat down next to Clementine. Earle unbuttoned his jacket and pulled at his tie, as if he couldn't take the stricture another moment.

"Wish you'd joined us today," said Agnes. "Reverend Willis gave a stirring sermon."

Clementine stopped Agnes before she gave her own full rendition of his inspiring words, unable to listen to God's word, even from Agnes. "How can you still believe in God after what he took from you?"

"Took from me?"

"Your legs."

Agnes looked down at her knees and smoothed her dress. "He didn't take away my legs. But he did help me deal with that loss."

"How can you not blame him for taking away your legs and then praise him for helping you deal with it?"

"God isn't responsible for all the good or bad that happens in this world."

"No, he's not. That's my point. What is he responsible for? Nothing. He does nothing for us."

Agnes reached for the little gold cross that she always wore, her fingers stroking its lines. Clementine instinctively reached for Finn's shell, twisting the silver chain that held it. Agnes sighed.

"I was angry for a while. I blamed the driver of that truck for going too fast. I blamed myself for running after Levi. I even tried to blame Levi for a bit. But sometimes accidents just happen for no reason. And it's my faith in God that helps me through those trials."

"My father believes that as well. When my mother died, he rejected practically everything except his faith."

"Faith truly can ease our burdens."

Did she visit him each night like she visited me? Before I slept, I felt my mother's kiss on my cheek. Until I left my father's house for good and left her behind as well.

Sin and forgiveness—both were Clementine's burden. "I don't even believe enough to reject God for taking away my boy. I have only myself to blame for that."

"Why all this need to blame?"

"I didn't know how to be a proper mother."

"No one knows how to be a *proper* mother. We all just do our best."

"Well, if that was my best, I don't deserve to be a mother."

"You know, Earle was so angry for a long time. Much longer than me, in fact. Helping him get over his anger helped me to be strong and move forward myself. I've learned to accept my injuries and adapt. I'm blessed with a wonderful marriage, a family. I'm happy with my lot." Agnes took Earle's hand and looked at the collection of family photos on the table. "You'll have the same someday."

Clementine thought of how much Earle adored Agnes and how difficult it must have been for him to forgive his God and still love him. Then she remembered Dorie's kind, sad eyes as she told Clementine about her daughter and how she had shut her memories and pain up in the dark.

Dorie tried to help me, and all I did was take and take.

Clementine cringed at the memory of torn paper littering the floor. She had destroyed the only tangible remains of Dorie's daughter. Shame flooded over her so that she felt shrunken. She reached for Finn's shell again and held it tight.

romeo

*d*orie sat on the deck doing a crossword. There was barely a breeze, and the late-summer heat was heavy and liquid. When the phone rang, she heaved her body off the chair as if moving in slow motion. It was Lynn.

"Izzie's missing."

Dorie's stomach dropped.

"She had a huge fight with Shel last night and then stormed out. Shel and Rennie are frantic. They have no idea where she is."

Dorie wondered if Izzie's girlfriend might have something to do with her disappearance. God knew what kind of trouble they were in. She interrupted Lynn's speculations. "I have to go."

"You know where she is?"

"Maybe. I need to talk to Rennie." She hung up and immediately dialed Rennie's number. It went straight to voicemail, so she jumped in the car and headed to his house.

He had on reading glasses when he answered the door and looked tired and distracted. "What are you doing here?"

"I just tried to call. We need to talk."

"Can it wait? I'm on my way out." He picked up an overnight bag and his car keys.

"Lynn told me Izzie disappeared. I think I might be able to help."

He stopped and looked at her. "You'd better come in, then. But make it quick."

Dorie couldn't help glancing at the large dining table as they entered his living space. It was covered in what looked like architectural drawings—sharp, straight lines and angles, indecipherable codes written neatly along the sides of each page.

Rennie sat in a nearby chair, his leg jiggling. "So . . . ?" He raised his eyebrows.

Dorie remained standing. "She's been seeing someone . . ."

"I knew it! She's been sneaking out all the time, skipping class."

"She was afraid of what people would think."

"Don't tell me she thinks she's in love. What, have they run away together or something? Is she going Romeo and Juliet on us?"

"Not exactly, no."

"Well, spit it out, for God's sake!"

"Just calm down, will you? This is exactly why she was afraid to tell you."

"Shit. She's pregnant."

"Rennie, stop. No. I think she may have left with . . ." Dorie searched her memory. "Kel, I think her name is."

"Kelly? That girl's bad news. But why would she run away with Kelly? They hardly know each other."

She couldn't tell him. Only Izzie could do that. "Just try contacting Kelly's family."

"Did you know she was going to run away?"

"Of course not."

Rennie looked at her in a way he never had before, with distrust. *So I've lost Rennie's trust to keep Izzie's.* Dorie pressed her lips together to prevent the whole truth from spilling out.

Rennie hastily gathered his belongings. "I have to go." He turned to the door and opened it, ushering Dorie through. Neither of them said another word as they each got into their respective cars and drove away.

edges of light

Clementine finished arranging the stack of envelopes she'd taken from Dorie's that terrible night. She organized them chronologically, starting with the ones she'd opened when they were first delivered years ago and ending with several that had remained sealed. Her journal sat next to them, the pages of which she'd been reading as though discovering her story for the first time.

She dug at the corners of her memory to find this young woman who had had so much happiness in her life. Joy that she'd taken for granted.

Clementine reached for the top envelope and slipped the page from the torn open edges. She reread the words she'd clung to so long ago, when Lou's letters were her sustenance.

Remember when you had nightmares and couldn't sleep? You'd wake me by stroking my face, so that I thought I was dreaming of walking through a forest, the trees brushing against me. I'd bury my nose in your neck until you nudged me further awake. Then I'd stroke your back and sing Johnny Cash into your ear until you fell asleep in my arms. I'm singing as I write this. I wish more than anything that I could feel you now.

I love you.

Lou

She picked up one of the sealed envelopes as if it were a locked box she'd hoped to forget, its contents something she had thought to leave behind forever:

His name's Jim. He's still in a coma, has been for several weeks now. I pray he'll come out of it. Every day, I pray. I pray for forgiveness for what I did. For who I am. I've been going to AA. They have a program here. It helps meeting guys like me, who have taken the wrong path. Messed up their lives. Lost those they love most. Are working on getting better. I'm working so very hard, Clem.

And another:

Jim's out of the coma. I wrote him, told him how sorry I was. He wrote back. He's a good man. I hope to be as good a man. He forgave me. Can you?

She tried to imagine the knot of words spilling from Lou's muddled mind, words that needed distance and time to get right, to convey the truth of his contrition as he attempted to climb out of who he was and into who he wanted to become. She had stacks of similar words.

And finally:

Clem, why didn't you tell me? Our beautiful son. I can't believe he's gone. I'm trying to understand why I had to hear it from the warden at the prison. I have to see you, talk to you. Are you okay? No, of course you're not. Please call or write. I need to hear from you soon.

Had Dorie read any of the unsealed letters? Her face hovered in Clementine's memory, a broken face that looked up at her from the shreds of Harriet's box on the floor. Clementine picked up the photo Lou had given her and stared at Finn's face. Then she headed to the barn.

Shafts of sunlight streamed through the high barn windows, muted by the grime and dust covering their panes, elevating the umber tones so the room was bathed in a rich golden light. Clementine strained to reach the upper edge of the canvas, every inch of which was marked with strokes of crimson and ocher merging with vivid hues of saffron and black. She moved her body like a dancer, swaying, lunging, arching, twisting, each muscle exerting itself. The brush was an extension of her arm as it dabbed, splattered, and smeared. Sounds rushed through her head and streamed out her fingers—the waves, the wind, the ocean—and she moved to their rhythms.

Her dark hair came loose, so she gathered it up impatiently and twisted, reaching for the nearest brush to anchor it. Hardly missing a beat, she resumed her dance. Her breath came quicker, harder as she started to tire, but she didn't stop.

Not yet.

Her palette knife gouged the harsh lines of the bush that was stripped bare of all but the monarchs' wings, never still. She captured their movements through grazes of color and knife edges of light. Clementine scraped and scuffed the surface of the canvas, altering the depth and tone to bring to life the flutter of those gossamer wings.

Juxtaposing the delicacy of a hundred butterflies with the life force of each one's will.

She was free, flying, watching herself from above. A young woman who no longer resembled who she once had been. A shaman conjuring an image of pigment and light to life, the memory of that moment. An interlude after their long journey. This refuge by the shore, a haven to gather strength, to renew, before beginning their life cycle once again.

splintered

When Lynn called to tell Dorie that Rennie had found the girls, Dorie was more than relieved.

"She went with that nasty girl Kelly to her cousin's in Beaumont. I don't know why she hangs around with her. She'll get Iz in all kinds of trouble. Apparently, they've been drinking and who knows what else."

Dorie listened to Lynn without interrupting, not wanting to tell her what she knew, what she'd kept secret for this misguided girl.

"I mean, I know Iz has been feeling overburdened, having to help Shel so much. But her poor mom just can't do it all on her own."

The child was bound to be punished by her mom, probably kept on an extra tight leash, which wouldn't help the situation at all. She just needed someone to talk openly with, someone who wouldn't judge her.

After they hung up, Dorie felt antsy. She decided a walk would do her good, so she put on her shoes and picked up her bag and keys. Perhaps not a walk after all. She wanted to talk to Rennie, to see how he was doing. How Izzie was.

When she climbed the stairs to his front deck, she found him sitting at a table outside, working on a contraption of some kind.

"I hear you found Izzie." He glanced up at her but continued tinkering. "I'm glad she's okay."

"I'm not sure she is." Rennie removed his glasses, looking like himself again. "Things aren't good right now." He looked up at Dorie. "Did you know?" Her throat closed up tight. "She told you?" he asked, his voice hardening.

"Told me?"

"About her and Kelly . . . being in a . . . relationship."

"No. I found them together. She was late to tutoring one day, and—"

"And you didn't think to share this with me?" His voice was not his own.

Dorie stiffened. "She asked me not to."

"Didn't you think it was something we needed to know anyway?"

She stood taller, her eyes narrowed. "Maybe if she trusted you more, wasn't afraid of your reaction, she might have told you herself."

Rennie stood up. "So Izzie's your latest project now? Are you going to try to save her next?"

Dorie clenched her car keys in her fist, felt the metal dig into her skin. She turned and walked away.

On the ride home, Dorie rolled down the windows, but the intense summer heat poured in, filling the air with a dense humidity that stuck to her skin and hair and clothes. She wasn't trying to save Izzie. The girl just needed someone to confide in, and her mother certainly didn't seem to be handling things very well.

Had Harriet kept things from her? Had she had secrets she was afraid to tell? Dorie imagined she would have been more likely to share them with Hugh than her.

Dorie suddenly felt the unbearable heaviness of regret.

A car full of rowdy passengers honked as it overtook her on the road, loud music careening off the boiling asphalt. She laid her hand hard on the horn, her blood surging.

She longed to rewind: back to before she moved to Bolivar. Before her marriage disintegrated. Before Harriet got sick. How far back would she have to rewind her life before she got to the good part, before it had splintered? It all seemed a lifetime away. Why were her days like lifetimes now, stretched behind her so that she felt an ancient sorrow without the wisdom that should accompany it?

She rolled the windows back up, cocooning herself inside her glass-and-metal shell.

open

Clementine stood outside the house that was once hers. Traces of him were there still, remnants that lingered in the call of the frogs, who had laughed with him in the rain. A breeze stroked her cheek, and she felt Finn in its fingers. But the house was Dorie's now, and she would leave her own imprint, and so on, and so on.

Until it was all finally claimed by the sea. As it should be.

When Dorie answered her knock at the front door, she froze and stared at Clementine, who stood in the rain, holding a large rectangular package covered in brown paper and string. "Clementine. What are you doing here?"

"This is for you." Clementine looked down at the wrapping, raindrops marking the paper with darker splatters, as if hinting at the gift inside.

Holding the door open wider, Dorie invited Clementine inside, watching her struggle with the gift for a second before helping her shift and angle it through the doorway. Dorie held it hesitantly, as if it were perhaps alive and she unsure what it might do to her. Slowly, she pulled the string and pushed back the paper, revealing the first glimpse of saffron and black. Then she removed the rest of the wrapping, uncovering the painting.

"It's that day on the beach," said Clementine. "When we saw the butterflies." Dorie nodded but didn't speak. "That's when I first knew that you understood me, perhaps better than anyone else."

"It's them. Harriet and Finn." Dorie's eyes brimmed with tears.

"Finn wouldn't have wanted me to stop painting. Once, he asked me why I painted. I told him it's how I love the world. He said he wanted to love the world by painting too and that we'd paint it together."

Dorie reached for Clementine, and they held each other quietly until the tears ran out.

precious

Shelley was shuffling the boys out the door when Dorie arrived. "Thank goodness you're here. Boys, quit dawdling; we're going to be late. Dorie, could you stay until I get back?"

"When will that be?" Dorie asked, feeling the tension in the room. Even the boys were quiet for once.

"Shouldn't be more than an hour, but you know how doctor visits can be." Chase sniffled and attempted to nuzzle into Shelley, with no success. "You mind Mrs. Edwards, Izzie," Shelley yelled from the stairs.

Izzie sat at the table, biting her nails.

"How are you?" Dorie asked, sitting down opposite her.

"Fine."

The girl looked so like the child she was that Dorie wanted to take her in her arms and stroke her hair, tell her how precious she was and that everything was going to be okay. But she hesitated to push her to open up if she wasn't ready.

"Let's get started with a warm-up exercise." Izzie pulled a piece of paper from the pile on the table and picked up a nearby pen. "Why don't you just freewrite today? Whatever you want. Ten minutes."

Izzie paused for a moment, then began scribbling frantically, head low to the paper. Dorie looked through the chapters they would discuss during the session but kept looking up at Izzie, who didn't stop writing for the entire ten minutes.

"Okay. Time's up."

Izzie looked up as if she'd forgotten Dorie was there. Then she wrote a few more words and put down her pen. She folded the sheet of paper twice and set it aside.

"So, I know you've been going through a lot lately, but did you find time to come up with some symbols that Harper Lee uses in the book?"

Izzie sighed and rummaged through more paper, looking for her homework. "I've been grounded indefinitely, so yeah, I had time." She pulled out a sheet and started reading from it.

The next hour was surprisingly productive, considering, though Izzie lacked any enthusiasm for their discussion. She seemed distracted, and Dorie had to coax out anything more than one- or two-word responses from her.

When Shelley walked through the door, Dorie was relieved. The session had been thick with unspoken words lying heavy in the air.

"How'd it go?"

"Pretty well," said Dorie as she packed up her things.

Shelley busied herself in the kitchen while Izzie followed Dorie to the door. As Dorie stepped outside, Izzie placed a folded piece of paper into her hand before walking away without looking at her. Dorie curled her fingers around the paper, running her thumb over the folds.

As soon as Dorie got into the car, she unfolded it. It was the warm-up exercise Izzie had written earlier. This was the first time she'd ever shared her personal writing with Dorie.

Someone wrote "dyke slut" on my locker door today. Kel said she'd find out who did it and get Nick to beat the crap out of them. Of course, me and Kel ran away—stuff like that happens all the time. Why do they hate me? I mean, I know why, but it doesn't make sense. When Uncle Rennie brought me and Kel back from Brenda's, none of us said anything during the car ride. He said it was Mom's place, not his. But when we got home, it was a nightmare! Mom was so mad!! I figured Dorie had already told them about me and that's how they found us at Brenda's. But she didn't. Cause when I told Mom I'm not ashamed of who I am, I'm not ashamed of who I love, she was so shocked! There's no way she already knew. I can't believe Dorie didn't say anything to Mom or Rennie. At least maybe someone is on my side and understands. Mom said I'm a sinner and she'll never be able to face anyone knowing what they know about me—I was so pissed! She thinks I'm doing it to get back at her. Like she has anything to do with this! I was kinda surprised when Uncle Rennie didn't yell at me or anything. He just hugged me and told me he loved me. He said Mom yelled cause she's worried about me and doesn't really mean it. I'm not so sure. I can't stand living with her anymore. When I asked Uncle Rennie if I could live with him, he said we'll see. I hate when grownups say that. It always means no. But I don't know how much longer I can stand this.

Dorie read it again before refolding it and tucking it into her pocket. She looked up at Shelley's house, but it was quiet and still, like an empty shell. Dorie wanted to run back up the stairs and into the house, grab Shelley by the arms, and shake her until she understood what was happening to her daughter. Just how close she was to losing her.

Lucille

Agnes knocked lightly on Clementine's bedroom door. "Someone's here to see you." Clementine got up and went to the front room. "Just holler if you need me," said Agnes as she went into the kitchen, which emitted enticing smells.

Dorie stood in the entryway, her arms cradling something close to her chest. "She's for you." Clementine heard soft mewls coming from the swaddled form as she came closer. Dorie carefully handed her the bundle. "She's the one that looks most like Rosie."

Clementine buried her face in the kitten's fur. Dorie stroked the kitten and then reached for Clementine's hand. "I'm sorry for not being a better friend."

Clementine squeezed her hand in return. "You're a perfect friend."

"I promised Rosie she could come visit, if it's okay with Agnes and Earle."

Clementine imagined Rosie and her baby chasing them all around Agnes's yard. Just as Finn had once done. "How do you get through each day without her?"

Dorie squeezed Clementine's hand. "She's always with me."

Clementine nodded. "The version they pulled from the sea that day, that wasn't Finn. And the version they handed to me in a metal canister afterward wasn't him either." She stroked Finn's shell with her thumb, remembering how the full moon had shone the waves silver the night she spread his ashes in the ocean.

Dorie touched her forehead to Clementine's, and they stood there, listening to the kitten purr.

"Anyone thirsty?" called Agnes from the kitchen. She wheeled into the front room, a tray on her lap.

Clementine put the kitten down on the floor, and they all watched her explore her new surroundings until she came back to them and rubbed against Clementine's legs, meowing for affection and love.

"How are the party preparations coming?" Dorie asked Agnes. Every year, Agnes and Earle invited the community over to celebrate the coming of fall and to share in their bounty. This year, Agnes had said it was extra special because Clementine had returned to them.

"Everything's under control. Should be able to get it all done by this weekend. I've got pots going on every burner. Everyone's bringing a little something, so I'm sure there'll be plenty of food. Even the grandkids are coming in. Should be here tomorrow morning."

Clementine could hear the excitement in Agnes's voice, could see the sparkle in her eyes as she anticipated her family's arrival.

"Who else is coming?" asked Dorie.

"Oh, practically the whole neighborhood, I reckon."

Clementine breathed long and slow, trying to settle her anxiety about being around so many people. She saw Dorie watching her and tried to smile reassuringly.

Dorie laughed. "Don't worry. You'll get used to it."

Clementine picked up the kitten and nuzzled against her, listening to her purr.

"What've we got here?" Earle walked through the front door and bent down to see the kitten in Clementine's arms.

"She's a new addition to the household," said Agnes.

"What's her name?" Earle rubbed the kitten's head, his large hand making her look even tinier.

Clementine paused for a moment. "Lucille." Her mother's name. "What do you think, *mi amo*?" The kitten purred even louder, her paws kneading Clementine's arm.

transformation

*d*orie needed to talk to Rennie. If she and Clementine were able to forgive each other, perhaps Rennie could forgive her too. A peace offering was in order, though. She went to the bookshelf and looked through the titles, settling on *Atonement*.

Too heavy-handed? What the hell. Everyone loves Ian McEwan.

When she pulled onto his street and saw his truck in the drive, she thought about turning around. He was probably still angry with her. Maybe she should give him more time. But her resolve took over, and she pulled up to the house.

It took him a while to answer after Dorie knocked, and she almost gave up and left. When he did eventually open the front door, he looked surprised to see her. *But happy surprised or annoyed surprised?*

"Hi." She tried to smile, but her lips twitched from nerves. "I brought you this book," she said, offering it to him.

He took it from her and turned it over to look at the title. Then he looked up at her quizzically. "Really?" She blushed. *Definitely too heavy-handed.* "Well, I guess I can give it a go."

The sun beat down on Dorie's back, and prickles of heat surfaced on her skin. "Rennie, I'm sorry about Izzie. You were right, what you said."

He opened the door wider, inviting her inside. They both sat down, and Rennie leaned forward in his chair, looking at her carefully. "I was worried about Iz and took it out on you."

Dorie was so relieved, she wanted to throw herself into his arms. But he probably hadn't forgiven her that much. "I'm just glad you found her and she was okay."

Rennie nodded. "Me too, me too."

"And how's Shelley?"

Rennie let out a puff of air. "I think she got so scared when Iz ran away that she's trying real hard to understand. So that's good, I guess. But she thinks it's a phase. Or hopes it is."

Dorie imagined that hadn't gone down too well with Izzie. "And you?"

"I'm just worried about what this choice will mean for her."

"I'm not sure it's a choice. It's just the way she is."

"You're right, I guess." He began picking at the edges of the book where they had started to fray.

I should have bought him a new copy.

"She's being bullied, you know." Rennie looked at Dorie then, his eyes so filled with compassion and sadness that she fought not to reach out to him.

Izzie's words on the page filled Dorie's head. "She'll need lots of support from people who care about her."

"She'll get that from me. We already talked to the school, and Izzie's seeing a counselor there. Not that she's too happy about it."

"I'm sure. That's good, though." Dorie looked down at her hands, clasping and unclasping her fingers. "Rennie, I promise I won't jeopardize her safety again by keeping anything serious from you."

"I'd appreciate that. Thank you."

Dorie hesitated, biting her lip. "She's begun showing me some of her writing. It's pretty personal sometimes."

"I get it. I don't expect you to tell me everything. Just the important stuff."

She smiled. "Okay."

"We're good, all right?"

Dorie nodded and breathed deeper. "Will you be at the Beauchamp's party this weekend?"

"Wouldn't miss it." Rennie's eyes lit up, and he looked at his watch. "Hey, what are you doing today?"

Dorie thought of time filled with walking and reading. "Nothing, really."

"We're going out on Pete's boat in a bit. You want to come?"

She imagined being on the water with Rennie, the wind forcing the air alive. "That sounds like fun. Sure, I'd love to come."

Dorie pulled onto a dirt track that wound through an overgrown lot to a lopsided clapboard house. Rennie and Pete were loading a small shrimp boat with coolers.

"Hi, Pete. Hope I won't get in the way today," said Dorie.

"Nah, you're good. We're almost ready to head out. Make yourself comfortable in the boat, if you like."

She'd only ever seen these vessels from afar, where they resembled bathtub toys bobbing on the water. Written in script along the hull were the words *Wayward Angel*. Dorie wondered for a moment what those words could mean to Pete.

The slap of a tinny door announced Lou's exit from the trailer. It was a relic from the 1980s, the brittle tan-and-brown plastic casing etched with cracks and gaps. Whatever tires it had once worn were long gone, and snaggletoothed blinds hung in the grimy windows. Lou approached the boat, glanced at Dorie, and quickly busied himself untying the lines.

They pulled away from the dock and soon reached open water, the low growl of the engine becoming a backdrop to shouts from the crew. Pete and Rennie tugged at cables, issuing instructions in a vocabulary Dorie didn't understand.

"Okay, lower the outriggers," directed Pete.

Huge metal arms raised in the air like a clumsy ballerina in fifth position, then slowly lowered into the water. Lou unhooked a clump of knotted threads and began to carefully unfold the net, each side bordered by weights and floats. They dropped the net into the water, where it dragged along the sandy bottom, scooping up shrimp gathered near the sea floor.

Rennie sat next to Pete, who lit a cigarette. "Hey, Pete, why don't you tell us about that time you almost caught a mermaid."

Dorie recalled Curtis's description of Clementine: *Long dark hair in waves. Like a mermaid, Leanne always said.*

Pete looked at them through the smoke curling around his head, pausing for dramatic effect. "I was in Florida, not too long after Hurricane Allison, fishin' with a buddy of mine. I reckon she musta got thrown off course or somethin'."

Dorie was already mesmerized by his melodic drawl and the gold hoop winking in his ear, just like as Lynn and her friends had been hypnotized around the campfire all those years ago.

"Course, I assumed I'd caught me a whopper of a fish, a shark even. I pulled on that line with all my strength, tryin' to get that sucker outta the water. She got close enough to the boat for me to see it weren't no ordinary fish."

Clementine *was* like a mermaid, a halfling—part myth, part human. At least, that's how Dorie used to see her. A tragic figure who needed to be rescued. Not a real person, living a life of both pain and joy, a life that could be fully lived.

Pete's voice reeled Dorie back into his story. "Now, you'd expect a mermaid to be a beauty, right? Shit, she weren't no beauty, I'll tell you that! Brown scales all over, bony arms—hands tugging at my line, trying to get loose—long fingers with sharp nails, like claws. Damn, she was ugly, more like one of them monster fish than human. But that fish had a face, I swear! Not much of a face, but she weren't no fish, that's for sure. I ended up cuttin' the line so she wouldn't pull me overboard."

Rennie piped up. "No telling what she'd have done with you!"

"Shit, she wanted me, man, but she weren't gettin' me. No way!"

"Damn, Pete," said Rennie. "You know what you should have done?"

"What?"

"You should have taken a goddamn picture—could be worth a fortune!"

"Humph, don't I know it." Pete shook his head and pulled a pack of cigarettes out of his pocket again. Everyone laughed, even Lou.

Dorie closed her eyes and sunned her face, the men's voices drifting in and out of her consciousness. A shadow suddenly blocked the sun, and she opened her eyes to find Lou standing over her.

"Dorie . . . how're things?"

She sat up, brushing her damp hair out of her face,

feeling hotter than ever. She tried to gauge Lou's tone. Did he know about Clementine staying with her all those weeks? Was he angry at her for not telling him?

"I want to apologize. For the way I acted at your house that day."

Dorie's stomach settled. "It was understandable, I suppose, considering the circumstances."

"Still . . . it won't happen again." Lou shuffled a little and took a draw from his cigarette.

Dorie wondered how many times he'd said that and hoped that maybe he meant it this time.

Rennie arrived at Dorie's side. "Here, you're looking a bit pink." He held out a tube of sunscreen. Lou nodded at Rennie before making his way back toward Pete. Rennie waited while Dorie applied some sunscreen to her face and then reached down to wipe a smudge of white off her nose. She felt sixteen again.

"Hey, Lou, wanna help haul it in?" Pete was moving again, pulling on a winch. They all circled around as he popped the bag lines to release the load, and an entire section of the deck overflowed with shrimp, the scent of the deep ocean filling the air.

They made another few runs, and Dorie took out the book she'd brought with her to pass the time. Instead, she found herself watching the men joking around as they hauled in the catch and stored it below deck. She thought of all the people she'd met since moving to Bolivar and how she'd assumed who they were before really knowing them: Clementine, the tragic figure she thought she could save but who ended up saving Dorie from shriveling up into a dark speck, showing her how to let herself care for someone again and to learn forgiveness. Lou, the ex-con who didn't deserve the woman he loved but who was transforming himself into a better man to try to earn her back. And Rennie, the good-for-nothing handyman who was slowly teaching her how to live again.

The sun sat lower in the sky, turning it a burnished gold. Pete told her they were heading back and opened some beers, handing them out to everyone. She noticed that Lou didn't take one, though he continued to smoke the whole time.

As Pete sat down, Dorie thought now might be a good time to indulge her earlier curiosity. "Why did you name your boat *Wayward Angel?*"

Pete swallowed what must have been at least half a beer before replying. "So I could keep a little piece of her with me, I guess."

"Who?" Dorie asked.

"Ah, she was a singer from around these parts."

"Would I have heard of her?"

Pete ignored Dorie's question and looked across the water, his body seeming to contract. "I knew her from school. We hung out behind the gym between classes, when we bothered to go to class, swiggin' whiskey and planning our escape. She was just this plain ol' thing, scrunched up face, crazy hair tamed into tight curls. Nothin' like the wayward angel she would become."

His voice was so low that Dorie found herself studying his face, trying to decipher the meaning between his words.

"I'd see her with either a sketchbook under her arm or a guitar slung over her shoulder. Half the time she'd dare you to mess with her, and the other half she'd stare at the ground, tryin' to disappear. But we knew she was one of us. We all started hanging out, partying, listening to music that weren't nothing like the crap those other kids called music. We did our own thing, man, didn't give a shit about those button-down short-back-and-sides freaks.

"She'd come to my house sometimes, and we'd get high. I played a Bessie Smith record for her one time—man, she flipped! That's when she started singin'—I mean, really singin'—none of that church choir bullshit. Goddamn, I never heard nobody sing like that—needles piercing your skin."

He drew on his cigarette and dropped his head. "That's when I fell hard."

Swarms of bickering seagulls followed the boat, hoping to grab an easy bite. Dorie watched them swoop and glide with murderous intent. She tried to imagine an awkward teenager from Texas transformed into the singer that Pete was describing. But then, perhaps everyone had the capacity for transformation. Dorie into a woman who could open herself up to the possibility of belonging. Clementine into a woman who had chosen to live.

Pete continued like a sleepwalker lost in a dream: "I remember one time, we were hanging at the beach with some kids from the colored high school. Some asshole started messin' with her, so she cussed him out and then went up to our friend Ellis and started makin' out with him all hot and heavy. I remember wishin' it were me. Anyways, some white preppy kid went up and pulled 'em apart, punched Ellis in the face. Man, you shoulda seen her. She went ballistic, beat the shit outta him! We were laughin' so hard, eggin' her on. The guy wouldn't hit her back, but still, he got rough with her. When he called her an ugly bitch, that's when all hell broke loose—best brawl I ever had—we always had the most fun hangin' with her. And I've had more than my fair share o' fun over the years, let me tell ya!"

The engine seemed to strain as the nets bulged with shrimp, dispersing its diesel scent into the sea air. "We were all a li'l bit in love with her. Tore me up when she left for

Austin. I followed her there, but I knew we'd lost her for good. She didn't have no time for me after a while. I hung around until she forgot who I was."

He looked around at them, abandoned by his memories. "So, that's how my boat got its name." Pete swallowed the last of his beer and threw the empty bottle into a bucket, where it shattered like a thousand broken lives.

Dorie thought of all the ways people kept those they'd loved and lost close. Stories, photographs, and physical manifestations, like Pete's boat and Harriet's box. And Clementine's pages, filled with endless words of beauty and pain.

epilogue

*t*he comforting aroma of freshly baked cakes that Dorie had made for the Beauchamp party permeated the house. It had transformed over the year that she had lived there. Harriet smiled back at her from shelves and tables around the room. Photos from the album, of which Hugh had made copies, now shared space with Clementine's painting, which hung on the wall between the windows facing the sea. Pieces of furniture Dorie had picked up at local antique shops settled into place among her existing possessions. The kitchen table sat center stage in front of the window, memories etched into its scars and crevices, so that Dorie felt a kinship with others who had left their imprint on this house, along with her own. The little yellow house by the sea was now a part of her.

Hearing the familiar rumble of an engine approaching, she glanced at her watch and smiled. He wasn't even late this time.

"Howdy, there," Rennie said as he reached the top step.

"Howdy, yourself."

He was carrying a large cooler. "For you—couple of redfish I caught and some shrimp."

"Thanks. Let's get them in the freezer."

His voice followed her into the house. "Whatever's cooking smells real good." He opened the cooler and started unloading its contents.

Dorie smiled, pleased to be cooking for this man who brought her offerings from the sea. To be cooking for her friends.

"You ready to go?" he asked.

"Almost done. Let me just pack up these cakes, and we can head out."

Rennie smiled at her. "You're finally getting the hang of beach time."

Dorie tutted but smiled along as Rennie started stacking the boxed cakes. She looked up at him and could see her joy reflected in his face.

They drove with the windows down, passing the last of the tourists soaking up the final month or so of summerlike weather that lingered into the fall. Three young children were building crooked sandcastles, directed by an older sibling. A group of children shrieked with pleasure as their kite caught the breeze and soared into the ether. Their mothers sat in the shades of colorful beach umbrellas, blossoms dotting the sand. Fathers swigged from their beers in between throwing horseshoes, their aim getting worse with each toss.

Beauchamp Ranch was alive with activity. The old live oak shook with glee as Earle pushed his middle granddaughter on the tire swing, her bare feet almost skimming the ground as she begged to go higher. Lou stood at a long table serving Lynn from a huge pot of chili, laughing as she flirted while glancing toward the barn. Rennie went into the house and was soon followed back out by Ken as they added more platters of food to the table. Agnes had her smallest grandson on her lap, giving him a ride in her wheelchair, much to his excitement. Shel was ordering Izzie to make sure Johnny and Chase didn't get the chickens too riled up.

That was when Dorie spotted Clementine by the barn. As she walked toward her, she noticed that Clementine's skin had lost its pale translucency; she looked more solid, grounded. She wondered what Agnes had done to bring her back to life. Something she herself had failed to do. The aura of sorrow Clementine had always worn had lifted some, and Dorie could see more clearly who she once was, who she could still become.

Dorie wrapped her arm around Clementine's waist, and they stood side by side in the September light that cast a muted glow over the people they knew and loved. They watched them play and bicker and laugh and cook and sing and dance. Dorie looked over to the bay side of the property with its stretches of open green fields, cows grazing lazily, flicking at flies with their tails, and eyeing their calves, who leaped like children playing tag. Tall reeds swayed along the waterway, and the sky teemed with birds, filling the air with friendly cries of recognition. When she turned back to Clementine, Dorie saw a glint of something in her face, sunlight reflected off water that she could almost miss if she blinked.

Rennie was talking to Ken, but he saw Dorie and came over. "Good to see you, Clementine. Mind if I borrow her for a while?" He gestured to Dorie. "Want to sit with me for a bit?"

She followed him to one of the tables on the periphery of the courtyard. He moved it out of the shade so that what was left of the waning sun could warm their backs. Dorie looked toward a ruckus coming from near the barn and laughed at the boys, who were chasing the chickens, which squawked with indignation.

"How's Izzie doing?" Dorie asked, watching her half-heartedly try to catch her brothers and redirect their attention to the swing.

Rennie nodded slowly, looking at Izzie with a combination of love and concern, deepening the furrow between his kind eyes. "She's staying with me for a bit. We'll see how she does. She had to promise her mother she'd still help out with the boys when Shel needs her. And wouldn't get herself into trouble, keep her grades up."

Dorie chuckled. "I'm sure she just loved that."

Rennie laughed. "Well, I figure it's worth a try." He turned his attention back to Dorie, his eyes still soft and kind. "She talks about you quite a bit. She trusts you."

Dorie smiled, a sense of ease spreading through her. "I'm glad. But it'll be a new challenge for you, I expect, having her live with you. It's a big responsibility to take on."

"You should know, right?" Rennie smiled. "Nah. It'll be nice having someone at the house again. Carl's doing real well with his music, so I don't reckon he'll be coming home for a long while. The house can get mighty quiet when it's empty."

"Very true." Dorie glanced over at Clementine and Lou, who were now sitting close to each other, the kitten between them. Lou kept leaning toward her, but right before they'd touched, he seemed to use all his will to force himself back. The narrow space between them shimmered.

Rennie followed her gaze. "You miss her?"

"Sometimes." The stillness and silence Dorie enjoyed now was because she chose it, when and how she wanted it. And perhaps she didn't want it quite as much anymore.

"This whole thing must have been difficult for you," Rennie said.

Dorie smiled. "Meeting Clementine was necessary."

"You do look more . . . I don't know . . . open? Happy, even."

Dorie realized that for the first time in longer than she could remember, it was true. "Moving here, meeting you . . . all of it was necessary."

The light was slowly fading, and the candles that Agnes and Earle had just lit glimmered, creating shadows that flickered and danced. It was the equinox, the time of year when day and night shared equal measure, hovering between light and dark, making Dorie long for more of each, uncertain of which she needed more.

"Thank you. For being my friend." She took Rennie's hand, feeling the lines and callouses, reading their meaning. "It was all easier, knowing you were here."

"You're very welcome. Any time you want me, I'm here."

Rennie's expression shifted slightly as Dorie leaned toward him. Then she kissed him, long and slow.

"So, we *can* be more than friends," he whispered into her ear.

"It seems so."

He smiled and put his arms around her, pulled her into him. She smelled paint and ocean air and something deeper underneath that she knew in her bones could become something she'd love. Dorie laid her head on his shoulder, and they watched the pink and orange brushstrokes of the Van Gogh sky slowly fade to reveal the shining stars. A billion lifetimes, lighting up one by one.

acknowledgments

my shiny bits:

Firstly, countless thanks to my publisher and advocate, Ynes Freeman, and to my wonderful and patient editor, Tod Tinker, at Balance of Seven press.

Eli, for making me stronger than I ever thought I could be.

Quentin, for making me a better writer and mother.

Joe, for making the possibilities boundless.

Mum, for listening to all my stories before anyone else, from the very beginning.

All my early readers: Simon, for reading a very early draft and managing to find the shiny bits. Lori—my forever friend who inspired all the shiniest bits of the women in this book. Sandra and Sarah, because you showed me how love, belief, and strength make it bearable (she is now a shining star in the sky). And Kathy, Kim M., Maria M., Kimberley, Suzanne, Michelle, and Tex, for all your encouragement and support.

Inprint, Writespace, Litopia, and Grackle and Grackle: inspiring fellow writers and teachers who make me a stronger writer.

And last, but not least, Bolivar Peninsula—a place of authentic beauty and real people that is now, and forever, a part of me.

about the author

Georgina is a writer and artist living in Houston, Texas, with her husband and two sons. She has an MA in English and has taught writing for many years: formally at the college level, through Writers in the Schools, and independently as a private tutor.

She and her husband are founding editors of the children's literary zine *Silver Rocket* and coauthors of the chapbook *Mean Ugly Cat*. She reads for Sight into Sound Radio and offers her voice talents for Litopia Pop-Ups. Georgina also volunteers at Writespace, a nonprofit literary arts organization.

After moving to the states from England, Georgina and her family would vacation in Galveston, Texas, each summer. Her dream of owning her own little house by the sea came true years later. The nearby community of Bolivar Peninsula was so different from where she'd been raised, but she quickly fell in love with the authentic beauty of the landscape and its inhabitants.

Shiny Bits in Between is her love letter to Bolivar Peninsula.

Visit her at georginakey.com for news and updates or on Facebook at Shiny bits in between.

CPSIA information can be obtained
at www.ICGtesting.com
Printed in the USA
LVHW081025060620
657509LV00009B/1118